SOFT ON SOFT

#FATGIRLSINLOVE

MINA WAHEED

CONTENTS

Book Cover Illustration and Design by Shafiq Shaar

Editing done by Melinda @ mute-editing.com

ISBN: 9781072890492

This is for fat anxious queer girls.

CONTENT WARNING

A content warning is necessary for discussion of a parent's death in inexplicit ways in chapter two, a depiction of a panic attack in the MC's point of view in chapter 8, usage of the word "bitch" endearingly, and discussion of anti-ace encounters in the past.

PROLOGUE

Selena hadn't believed in love at first sight. Had the concept existed? Sure. Had she thought she would ever experience it? Probably not. The whole idea of instant attraction hadn't seemed *for* her. But appreciation totally had been something she enjoyed. She had loved looking at people. Their dynamics and appearances all had fascinated her.

It was one of life's biggest blessings that her daily life had included meeting people who were vibrant, unique, and attractive. And not just what society had deemed attractive.

All around Selena, the world had burst into colors, and laughter, and positivity.

As a fat model, she had done photoshoots with other cis fat women, who had looked like her. The women had been soft around the middle and outspoken about giving fat people a voice in a world that didn't care.

As a black woman, Selena had worked with other black people who were all hues of melanin. It had been where Selena felt the most like home. Like when she'd been around her sisters and mom. Their talk and their mannerism had pulled Selena into a safe zone.

As a queer woman, Selena had cracked jokes about her demisexuality with people on the rainbow spectrum. With them, Selena hadn't needed to open a PowerPoint presentation of how her attraction worked. They'd just understand.

Through past year or so, Selena had felt the same way around June Bana. Even if Selena hadn't had a clue whether June was even attracted to female-coded people. Selena knew her attraction to people, as complicated as it felt at times, was also simple. It required Selena's emotional engagement and with June, engagement came so easy.

The freckled fat makeup artist was all kinds of intriguing. From how little June posted about herself, to how her page sometimes exploded with the intimacy in every stroke of eyeliner.

For Selena, she had to adopt a new form of Love at First Sight. Selena called it Love at First Makeup Collaboration. And that's how Selena discovered so much about herself.

Like in everything in Selena's life, she pursued it by working hard and getting enough beauty sleep.

It was only Selena's nature to pursue the tingle in her chest that travelled so far down her body that it got her toes to twitch.

The tingle acted as Selena's signal. She listened to it.

It rang keenly when Selena entered the venue for the photoshoot and made her way to the makeup corner. Selena felt time freakishly slow down at seeing June's outline in the distance, seeming to have a glow about her, making every particle of her curly hair stand out.

When Selena's hands shook for the first time ever at meeting June Bana, Selena took a breath and reminded herself that she was in control. After all, Selena had felt a certain level of confidence walking in. She had her favorite ensemble on. If one wanted the confidence of one Selena Clarke, one always donned something floral.

Yet in that moment, when their hands had touched to shake, it hadn't felt like Selena was in control at all. It had felt like fate was.

Is this what the romance Japanese comics Joey and I read in college were talking about? Selena had thought senselessly.

As if on autopilot, Selena's easiest smile had taken over her and Extroverted Selena had been in charge. Maybe Selena had laid on a little bit more charm than necessary. Maybe, when over the two hours that Selena had sat in June's makeup chair, she had allowed fate, the cruelest thing, to accelerate her heartbeat and entangle her emotions into a nice little bundle of wires.

Fate might be powerful, but Selena Clarke was even more powerful. She knew her strengths. She chitchatted, picked at June's brain, and made June laugh even if it was a quiet affair with a minimal amount of exhaled breath and a smirk.

It felt like victory when Selena called June *cool* and the freckled face turned a crimson so beautiful no brand could ever mimic. Selena's treacherous heart, which calmly had said *hmmm, beautiful* about every one of Selena's previous significant others, practically shot out of its cage.

It all made sense to Selena then. She liked this girl. This freckled, round cheeked, focused girl. Everything about June, or what Selena could glean in those two hours, made Selena want to know more. Looking back at it, Selena probably had been very much into June, but was held back by the impenetrable wall June had had around herself.

Selena had admired people before. She was well-aware

of the exciting first days of dating someone. That feeling in the pit of Selena's stomach sang to it. The tightening with every intense stare June gave her –and June stared a lot. (Well, June had to. She was doing Selena's makeup after all.) The way Selena's eyelids couldn't stop from fluttering whenever June's mouth quirked in that semi-smile-but-mostly-smirk movement.

Stepping out from that chair didn't stop Selena. She had been drawn to June's direction. Selena sneaked looks at June while also concentrating on giving the photographer the pensive gazing and the perfect pouts they kept asking from Selena.

Late that night, or morning depending on how finnicky people were, Selena laid back in her bed, in a pitch-dark room, and scrolled through BANAJOON, a feed of June. A feed of color, minimal captions, and the occasional cat picture or two. When Selena caught herself leaving the fourth comment in a row, she realized something. One, Selena was very very direct, and obvious. Two, she was crushing.

Massively. Kind of intrusively. But it was all together exciting and heart-stopping.

CHAPTER ONE

June Bana knew two fundamental truths.

One, she was not immune to Selena Clarke's charm. Fighting the full smile and twinkling brown eyes in a face so sweet had been impossible a year ago and was nearly excruciating that very minute.

Two, someday, a day she would get over the twist of anxiety in her stomach, a day that felt like today, she was going to say, "fuck it," and get in all kinds of trouble with her self-control.

Selena S. Clarke (the S could stand for every adjective under the sun; Sweet; Sexy; Scrumptious) was everything one could imagine from an Instagram model that rose to power thanks to her honesty, grace, positivity and—June thought with a dreamy sigh—how knockout gorgeous she was.

The power of one Selena smile was akin to staring directly at the sun. Pretty damn strong. Right then, she had perched her lovely ass in June's makeup chair and outright flirted with her. While smiling.

If there was another thing besides Selena's glowing

smile that weakened June's knees, not counting all her social anxieties, it was flirting.

"Your freckles are seriously the most amazing thing I've seen. How come you never show them off? I can predict around twelve hundred comments all starting with, 'Oh dear freckled goddess, please—'"

June couldn't help herself, she smiled. Selena, as if astonished that she did, paused. Her grin got even bigger.

"I prefer you being the only star," she murmured as she brushed out the black model's luscious brows. Usually, she preferred a pretty quiet makeup session, but she never had a problem doing Selena's most intricate details—like her eyebrows—as the model chatted livelily.

"I'm just saying, Junie—" There was also that nickname that made June's heart flutter in her chest. "—we'd make a good team."

Then she winked.

Again, Selena shouldn't have done that, but she didn't mind. She had something to focus on besides the litany of *holy shit, she's cute*, in her brain. Plus, her best friend, Shelby, was fidgety, but she always managed.

"I don't do well behind a camera that's not my own," she said as a way of explanation.

Selena looked contemplative. "I get it. You're a perfectionist."

The words were so true, she simply shrugged. She usually wasn't this reactive with people. She gave a smile, maybe a little "Hello, how are you doing?" that was casually answered. Her focus went into making sure everything she was asked to do was done perfectly. Just as Selena surmised.

But with Selena, she just found herself opening-up. Like a shy little blossom. She wanted to scoff at her own thoughts, but she saw herself in the mirror sometimes. She saw how her blush spoke paragraphs, with a generous number of freckles that flared up whenever she couldn't handle any of what Selena was offering.

And Selena knew her effect on her. Didn't stop the model. The flirting never felt too much, though. Somehow, Selena had gleaned her limits.

But sometimes Selena would wink and turn her into putty into her hands for as many hours as a shoot required them to orbit one another. Make her laugh with exaggerated model poses. Offer to help carry her things, which on more than one occasion made her parade her "muscles." And in the end, gave her a good time.

She was a wreck, and Selena knew but never pushed.

Selena smiled and closed her eyes, letting her get back in her groove. She brushed, drew, buffed out, smeared, and spritzed until Selena's dark skin glowed as if a light had been lit up within her. Her lips especially were June's favorite bit. They were a bright pink with a brown ombré that drew attention to the very center of Selena's luscious lower lip.

Her hair had already been taken care of by Jackie. The six feet tall black hair-stylist scared the shit out of everyone but was always her fluffiest around Selena. June also knew it was 110 percent Selena's effect. She'd seen Jackie around some real jackasses in the small community they shared.

Jackie was the best and anyone would be lucky to have her touch their hair.

Jackie's touch was magic. She gave Selena's curls life, shine, and room to bounce off her shoulders. Her shiny shoulders.

Very faintly, June heard the speakers around them play *I Will Survive* and just the title felt like a joke. She would not survive. At all. She would crumble at the very shake of Selene's shoulders. Happily.

"We're done," June murmured.

She wasn't much for words and usually met her quota by three in the afternoon. It was pushing on nine and she was both wired and tired from adding little flowers to Selena's body.

She especially felt an incredible jealousy of the burst of pink flowers that gathered around Selena's neck. Her lips tingled with an urge to do something that didn't involve speaking. Selena hummed along to the song under her breath.

When Selena saw her reflection, her mouth fell in a little perfect *oh*. As if the fact that she looked mesmerizing was entirely new. With the bright green eyeshadow required for the theme, her eyes glowed like honey. The transformation included some body paint done in florals of pink and white and shades of red that turned her into a wood fairy with whom June wanted to spend all her days.

"This is so amazing," Selena said. With awe painted all over her face, she dragged the vowels in her mouth as she inspected how the blush blended seamlessly into some of the flowers had created an eye grabbing illusion.

"This is great, June, Jackie." Brianna, the coordinator of the shoot, came bustling in. Her mouth was set in a permanent grin and it looked even wider now. June felt the exhaustion second-hand.

June nodded along but her mind refused to pay attention. It was about the shoot, but she'd attended two other meetings and doubted she'd miss something crucial.

Besides, her attention was focused on Selena who had whipped out her phone and was taking selfies. They were probably for her thousands of adorers. Followers who could tell her "YOU'RE GORGEOUS," "I LOVE YOU" and "DATE ME!!!" without turning thirteen different shades of pink.

June peeled her eyes away. She was so weak.

To distract herself, she began to clean up. Shelby usually tagged along to take care of that, but the poor pal had a chest cold and had to stay home. June missed them. Shelby got June's quiet nature.

By the time she came out of her concentrated haze of putting everything she wouldn't need in her giant cases, Selena was already ushered away where she posed with props that fit the theme.

It was for a makeup brand. She enchanted by how the light adored Selena. Between shots, Selena would shake her hips to whatever song played. At that minute, it was *Holding Out for a Hero*. June laughed as she sang along. She got yelled at for twirling around and kicking one of the props out of its spot.

As if hearing her laugh, Selena turned to her and began to mouth lyrics. June's heart ached. She leaned against her station and watched.

The energy Selena came with was obvious in every move and new outfit. She counted not one but four changes that the wardrobe people fussed over. She was asked for some minimal edits, an alteration or two to the look, which she was happy to comply with.

What she wasn't happy about was how the bright lights waned some of Selena's excitement, but every new song made her burst into dance.

June wondered just how much sunshine one person could store.

Someone was definitely feeling the *Shrek* mood. She gave Selena a nod and swiftly got out of everyone's hair.

The photoshoot ran smoothly for most of its duration, but like any standard operation that required a team of professionals, it went on longer than expected. By the time June shook hands with waved goodbye to Brianna, it was nearly two a.m.

She wasn't the only one feeling the exhaustion. By the end, Selena's dance moves had turned sluggish. When the shoot wrapped up, Selena gladly got out of the spotlight, shaking hands and exchanging cheek kisses. When she got to June's makeup and hair area, her shoulders visibly dropped. She hurried behind a divider to change her clothes.

"Good job, there," June murmured when Selena reappeared. She handed Selena a bottle of water.

Selena took it with a grateful smile. "I'd kill for some tea right now."

"Tea at this hour?"

"Yeah, tea is the one drink I would never say no to. Except if a white person offered," Selena explained. She sniggered.

Jackie came then to remove all the flowers and other plant stuff they got safely glued to Selena's skin in the process of shooting. Selena tried to help. Keyword being "tried." Except she was drowsy and mostly just made jokes. Jackie swatted her hand away a couple of times, but she smiled softly and continued her attempts at helping.

June watched.

Once the prosthetics were off and Jackie hugged Selena goodbye, Selena started on removing her makeup.

"Here, let me help," June murmured.

She felt a bone deep ache in her back, but she couldn't let Selena struggle with the makeup all by herself. Plus, she had some industrial makeup wipes that'd help greatly.

She handed Selena one as she used another to clean up the glitter from Selena's shoulders.

"You don't have to, Junie, I can guess how exhausted you must be. No matter how many *Shrek* songs they play, we still get tired," Selena said. Her voice was its usual soft cadence. She absent-mindedly smeared the mascara rather than cleanly wipe it off.

Done with shoulders, June stepped towards her face. She made sure she used short gentle swipes as she removed the remnants of the black that collected under Selena's eyes. When she got some errant glue off Selena's cheek, Selena gave her a soft smile.

Selena's mouth was in its usual curl. Her mind, for a minute there, wondered if it'd taste as lovely as it looked. Then she told herself to fuck off and stop being fixated.

She got distracted by the flutter of Selena's lashes. There was something there. She leaned in. She saw the piece of glitter there that probably irritated Selena. June cupped Selena's cheek. Her eyes widened at the proximity. June's heart thumped. She brushed her thumb under Selena's left eye, taking with it the devious bit.

June took a big deep breath and stepped back. She shouldn't have done that. It brought to mind Selena's scent. Almond and vanilla. She hadn't been any closer than she'd normally be to apply a tricky detail, but the closeness still made her heart riot. It didn't help that she noticed the erratic rise and fall of Selena's ample chest. Even back in a white shirt and blue jeans, she appeared edible.

June thought her heart would betray her and physically manifest to snuggle in the juncture between Selena's neck and shoulder. The thought made her unconsciously smile. She remembered she was terribly awkward and fiddled with the used napkin. Selena cleared her throat. June looked up and saw an indecipherable look on Selena's face.

"So, do you have plans next week?"

She ran through her mental schedule. She had three days free from her part-time job at the Salon by her mother's bookstore. Selena brightened when June told her.

"Excellent! There's this party I'm hosting on Friday for my best friend's baby shower. I'd love if you could come," Selena said. June saw her biting her lower lip. She didn't think she would ever pose as a reason for Selena to be self-conscious.

June mentally asked her anxiety: *would this be okay?* After being bathed in Selena's glow, anxiety usually calmed the fuck down, so June was not surprised at the quiet in her mind.

"Okay." It felt so simple to say *yes*. To say yes to potential. Her heart rejoiced but her stomach plummeted as if anxiety just woke up then. But June didn't care. With anxiety plaguing her every minute of the day, she'd expected it, to be frank.

"That's great! I'll DM you my location," Selena said. Her eyes had been a bit half-cast and exhausted but now they were open with excitement.

"It's at your place?"

"Yep! I'm going to be the most adorable host."

June smiled. She had no doubt about it. She also said that bit aloud. Selena batted her lashes and waved a hand at her in faux-shyness.

June had never been to Selena's house before. She'd done her makeup dozens of times over the past year but never at a place as intimate as Selena's. She was kind of, sort of, just a teensy bit, anxious.

"I can't wait," June said. And every bit of that sentence was true.

THE APARTMENT BUILDING WAS SURPRISINGLY NOT that big. June could even see its top level. Huh. She didn't know what to expect but maybe something that disappeared into the clouds. Something befitting a fairy like Selena.

She easily found a parking space which was another sign Selena's neighborhood was unlike hers. The chill made her shake in her lightweight jacket. She was the kind of person who'd go out in February without precautions. June thanked god her jeans were nice and snug though. Which totally was not because she wanted Selena to notice her thick ass. Not at all.

With one final hoist of her purse strap, she walked inside. The doorman seemed prepared for guests and once she showed him the invitation Selena had cutely made, he ushered her to the elevators.

June rode an elevator to the thirty-eighth level. She prayed it didn't suddenly stop. Her stomach was excited and nervous, which was she used to. She'd never lived in a building with a functioning elevator before.

She checked the text message with the information probably fifteen times before she pressed the doorbell on apartment 38-b. June heard the echo of faint music. The bass was subtle, and the lyrics were crooned by a low voice. None of that mattered when Selena opened the door.

She absently thought, there should be fireworks. Why aren't there any fireworks? Oh yeah. They're in my chest.

Selena wore a baby-pink wrap dress. It hugged her wide

hips, plumb belly, and full chest. It left her shoulders bare. June swallowed harshly. *Uh-oh, let the thirst begin.*

"Junie!" Selena's voice did wonders to her stomach. She smiled. She'd been saving her daily quota of smiles and thought now was the perfect opportunity to use one. Again, the same feeling of ease washed over her. Smiling for Selena filled her with warm homely feels, like when she fed her cats.

"Selena. You look gorgeous." The words rolled off her tongue so quickly she couldn't hope to stop them. Selena smile went wide. *Uh-oh,* June's insides warned, *we're under attack.*

Oh, shut up, we're always under attack. This attack is certified. Welcomed. Happy to be received, she retorted. What anxious person didn't shout at their source of usual fear and despair?

"Thank you. You too." June beamed.

She didn't miss the long look Selena gave her. Did June maybe put an extra effort to impress her? Yes. It didn't hurt that Selena's look was a once-over that didn't try at subtlety.

Thank god it didn't because the look poured little tingles of joy into June's heart.

Under her jacket, she had on a blue and pink checkered shirt French tucked into black skinny jeans. Her hair was pinned back in a loose bun. She'd left her face bare. She didn't mind that her skin was spotted with acne scars. It took her a long time to love them and she didn't cover them. Besides, she was proud of her dusting of freckles.

"Here, I got your friend a present. Hope that's okay." Selena smiled at the small yellow packaged gift. It was a pair of tiny shoes. They were so unfunctional and minia- ture. She'd seen them two hours into her browsing.

Selena welcomed her inside and took her jacket. June

accepted the pair of slippers she offered. She led June down a long hallway lit by soft yellow fairy lights. The glow, combined with the low-light of the place, threw shadows around that calmed the senses. For minute, June's anxiety forgot that she was supposed to be meeting more than three people that night.

She envisioned something different. Something along the line of sipping Sprite and sneaking a hand into Selena's hair. The imagined sensation of the curls in her fingers made her visibly shiver. Selena threw her a look over her shoulder as she led them to the living room. That dried up June's throat. The sight of Selena's shiny curls, some atop her head and some falling softly against her bare neck and the tips of shoulders, was pure art. The curls looked defined and arranged so beautifully. Like a bouquet.

Someone should save June from her brain.

They passed the kitchen with its assortment of refreshments and snacks laid out on the counter separating the open space.

Selena stopped there and spread out a palm in the universal sign of "Help yourself."

June saw a can of Sprite and in an act to maybe make her fantasy come true, she snatched it. It was cool against her sweaty palms. She took sips as Selena chattered about how she'd spent the last three hours covered in wrappers from the decorations. The place was a mix of incredible pink balloons, bright and sparkly blue ribbons, yellow lights.

"As you can clearly see, I... uh, might have gotten defeated by the image in my head and... I am not as color coordinated as you might expect from someone with an Instagram feed that consists of pastels," Selena sounded sheepish.

June shook her head a couple hundred times. Selena's mouth got wider with each shake until she was beaming.

"This is so lovely. It's so intimate and…" she trailed off, her fingers itching to touch the lights Selena had hung from the ceiling.

How did she get that far up ahead? When June turned, she saw Selena enveloped by the lights, her skin glowing and her eyes glimmering with something besides her usual playfulness. "Spontaneous," June finished her thought.

Selena wrung out her hands, but she smiled beautifully at June's comment.

"Well, you're kinda early hence why we're the only people."

June blushed at that. She couldn't help but show up either twenty to forty-five minutes early to any plan. It was a basic survival trick to always being anxious. And she said as much to Selena.

"Uh, that's relatable as heck so don't worry. Joey is on her way with her wife!" Selena said. "Besides, I have an idea for how we can spend the time."

She'd added the last with an especially flirtatious curl to her mouth.

After nine months of basking in the glow and flirting of one Selena Clarke, June could archive and label every smile that mouth pulled on her. Which was pure science. Totally not June's fixation on Selena's mouth. Absolutely not.

"That sounds scary and frankly, I'd let you do whatever you want," she explained with a shrug.

As if by magic, June's words activated Selena's smile to a whole new level of mind-blowing lovely. Also, it didn't hurt to see Selena's lashes flutter against her full cheeks.

CHAPTER TWO

"How long have you known Joey?"

"We graduated the same class. She basically saw me crying in the bathroom one day my second year of college and we became friends," Selena professed. She was in the process of decorating tiny cupcakes.

"Wow, that long?"

"Yep, it's been close to eight years." She looked up from scrutinizing the last tiny cupcake in her current batch. It was a beautiful peachy color. She'd made so many of the small things, June had lost count. She sipped her Sprite. A thin layer of shine on one corner of Selena's forehead made her fingers tingle to lean over to blot it.

"It's cool that you got to meet a best friend in college. First year, I was struggling to balance shit out. What with me being anxious and my father passing away," she blurted. Automatically, she wanted to take back the oversharing.

"I'm sorry to hear that," Selena murmured. She paused her decorating, but June automatically shrugged.

"I was diagnosed three months after my father passed

away. I got on meds and it was a journey but I'm as balanced as I could be," she murmured. She sounded so self-deprecating. God.

Selena nodded at that and June was relieved that she didn't ask about her father. It'd been eight years since Baba passed away but no matter how many times June mentioned it, it never got easier to talk about it. In those first two years, she'd used to crack one joke after the other. Using humor as a shield had been her go-to solution to ignore her emotions for a long time.

June recalled how she stood in front of her mirror and made lots of promises to be anything but herself, she decided: fuck it. She was going to roleplay as a more courageous version of herself.

"It helps that I have two roommates who masquerade as alarm clocks and keep me accountable. Who basically lick my lashes to get me out of bed." She tried to lighten up the mood although Selena hadn't looked very uncomfortable. She was quite focused on her cupcakes, adorably so.

"Your cats, right? Lemon and Mint, yeah?" Selena worked methodologically. June could see how steady her hands were. How she held her breath for a couple of seconds as she perfected every dollop of cream on the cupcakes.

"Yeah! Lemon and Mint. My kids." As if on autopilot, June whipped out her phone from her purse.

She realized then that she hadn't touched it for the past fifteen minutes she'd been at Selena's. That must have been some sort of millennial achievement, right?

She brought up pictures of her cats. June knew Selena had probably seen one or two of the thousands of pictures she posted of the dynamic feline duo, but June had two topics she loved talking about the most: her cats and makeup.

"Lemon is older and grumpy but so, so, so loving. He—he's usually the one waking me up. Mint is around a year now and I got him the beginning of the year when I needed a heavier weight to keep me grounded."

She hadn't told anyone that. People knew generally that Lemon was older due to how long she'd posted his pictures but not about Mint. Not about the reason of why she adopted him the minute a friend of a friend from school had posted about her cat giving birth to a litter of mixed breed kittens.

Selena paused her cupcake-decorating, washed her hands quickly, and leaned over the counter, which brought her gorgeousness so much closer, making June stutter one or three hundred times. Thankfully, Selena was intent on the phone and drying her hands. She probably didn't see the thirteen shades of enchanted June had turned into.

Selena busily cooed and hummed at June's words. She reached with a clean hand and asked with her eyes, "Is it okay if I swipe?"

June nodded. Her camera roll was full of cat pics, reaction pics, makeup looks she'd done at her part-time, and looks she'd done on herself.

Selena's eyes brightened with every swipe and June didn't feel the usual dread of people reacting to the innerworkings of her chaotic brain. She stopped at a picture that June snagged when Lemon had perched on her chest and Mint was sniffing her cheek.

"You look so adorable," Selena admired.

"Maybe a family can be one Arab-Persian bum and her two cats."

"Bum, pfft," Selena huffed jokingly, and June shrugged. She was self-deprecating. It was part of the package.

Selena raised an elegant eyebrow. "So, Persian huh? I didn't know that. I mean, I knew you were Middle Eastern, but–"

"Not a lot of people know because, uh, I can't really speak Persian. Apparently, that's a good enough reason to revoke my ethnicity to some people." The last might had been influenced by a bitter encounter or two she'd been through.

"Some people can choke," Selena said. June smiled. Just like that, Selena could say or do something, and June would find herself shrugging whatever brought her down off her shoulders.

"Choke they shall. Anyway, yeah, dad was Persian, and my mom is Arab. She owns a bookstore."

"That's cool. Did you grow up basically between the bookshelves?" Selena came across a picture of June sitting in a section of Bastoog, surrounded by books. June had liked the picture a lot but now she basically wanted to frame it for the way Selena's eyes twinkled as she stared at it. After a minute, Selena gave her the phone back.

"Kind of? My mom was busy most of the time, but we had a close neighborhood of other Arabs, so I grew up surrounded by people who knew my mom and knew me my whole life."

"Do you still live with your mom?" Selena asked. She went back to sprinkling a decent amount of edible sugar flakes on the cupcakes.

"Uh-no. Not for a while. I had a roommate for a while but, yeah—I rent an apartment with my cats."

Absently, she realized that the conversation had consisted of her spilling a lot of information and the imbalance made her want to smack herself across the head. She wanted to know if Selena also grew up reading. If she had a favorite relative.

"What about you? No pets?"

Although Selena was quite open with her life on social media, June didn't assume. Being protective of her privacy meant June kept so many things off her page. She didn't feel comfortable or ready to let people into every facet of her life.

Selena pouted a little as she said, "No. I used to take care of the family dogs but since I moved in this place and I've been too busy to actively take care of anything but myself."

"That's cool. I mean taking care of yourself is essential."

Selena smiled. "Well, it's a challenge. Speaking of, I'm visiting my mom sometime soon thanks to a little break in my schedule. Spending a week back home and everything."

June perked up. "Does this mean pictures of you with dogs?"

"Probably." Selena laughed as June gave her a pleading look. "Okay, yes, sure."

It was her secret weapon and phew, it worked. Okay, so June might get the hang of this whole putting herself out there and ignoring her anxiety shouting she's boring all the god damn time.

"What's your favorite thing about your mom?" She thumbed the can in her hand.

Selena took a minute to thing. "I guess I like how hard she loves. Despite my mom's old age, she had me when she was in her late forties, she was generous with understanding. She made sure I knew she loved me unconditionally."

The song in the background changed to something June was familiar with. Sza crooned in 20 *Something* and as

Selena busied herself with cleaning up any mess that happened thanks to the cupcakes making process, June got comfortable with the idea that she adored Selena.

"I've got to admit. It was a bit of a powerful move to invite you tonight."

June leaned back unconsciously. Did she come off as... mean? The thought horrified her until Selena shook her head at whatever went on June's face.

"No, no, no, not like that." She shook her hands.

"Oh?" June took measured breaths to calm her facial expression.

"It's just that... We kind of are friends, right?" the hesitation in her voice tugged at June's heart.

"Yeah, totally," she murmured. There was no hesitation.

At that, however, Selena seemed to blossom even more. She beamed. "That is such a relief to know. It's always very tricky for me to, like, know if the people I see occasionally are actual friends or just... acquaintances." She was rambling. June never saw Selena ramble. It was kind of surreal.

"I totally get it."

"So, yeah, I wanted to introduce my friends to the mastermind behind some of my best looks for campaigns and stuff. I mean, by now, I'm sure all of them would think I made you up if it wasn't for your Instagram page. But I didn't know if you'd be comfortable with that sort of thing. If you only saw me as a work kind of person."

June tucked her chin into her chest. She felt so weirdly happy to be the recipient of Selena's praise. And to occupy some space in her thoughts.

"And like, being my annoying self and being ace, well, demisexual but you probably don't know what that is—"

"I do," she interjected. Because holy shit, Selena was demisexual.

Selena seemed to shine even brighter. "You do? That's so cool."

"I mean, I am pansexual. Us on the end of the acronym gotta stick together, right?" Selena blinked back in surprise. June actually came out on Instagram, but it was a long time ago and many people kind of didn't notice it.

"Yeah! Totally!"

They giggled.

"This is surreal. I usually must explain. Most often it's to allosexual cis het people but it's also nice that another queer—Sorry, is it okay if I use that word for you? I've reclaimed it, but I shouldn't assume you have too."

"Oh, yeah, absolutely. I don't mind."

Selena huffed in what looked like relief. June knew how that must feel like so well.

"So, as I was saying. Making friends is a big deal to me 'cause lots of people think I can make them easily but, considering my career choice? Nuh-uh." June was enchanted by both the hurried way she was trying to get the words out. It involved a lot of hand moving, which meant she fidgeted with a thin necklace that nestled in her collarbones. June wanted to kiss Selena's nerves away.

"So, yeah, I wanted to know you better and at the same time stop my friends from thinking I'm making you up. And look it, party hasn't even started, and I already know so much."

"I know, yikes," June couldn't help herself from muttering jokingly.

Selena chuckled at that. "Hey, you're okay. I'm the one oversharing. I'm a chaos."

"A pretty chaos," June blurted. Holy shit, where did the

strength to say that come from? And could she have more, please?

"Flatterer." Selena's eyes turned half-mast at that, making June feel the pulse in her own throat. Going a bit wild.

"Nah, just honest," she murmured.

"You know, usually, people use that for when they're being jerks. I'm glad people like you exist who use it for kindness."

June shrugged, she knew she was blushing so hard she looked like a ripe tomato. Selena's grin turned even sweeter. They settled into a nice comfortable silence as June watched Selena bring out even more hors d'oeuvres.

The quiet was interrupted with the sound of the door unlocking and footsteps. "Selena," came the call from the hallway. June braced herself. Two people come in with even more food and cautious hugs.

Selena introduced June to her Joey, who was a tall, round, and striking Pakistani person with a black dress on with tiny baby pugs at the hem.

"Your dress is adorable," June commented.

Joey grinned. "Thank you, it was the first thing Selena gave me when I told her I was pregnant."

Then, a person wrapped a multi-rings adorned hand around Joey's own long fingered hand. Joey smiled softly and said, "This is my spouse, she's nonbinary, and uses she and her pronouns." The beautiful black person that came next to Joey smiled.

"Hi, I'm Noor." Noor was shorter than Joey, with dark brown skin, and a shaved head. She wore thick-framed glasses and a teal pigment that made her brown eyes look beautiful. She shook June's hand and with every second,

June fell in love with the soft looks the couple would give one another.

"I'm June." Just then, Selena showed up from the kitchen with a bunch of pins in a tiny basket.

"Here, I forgot to put these out. I got preoccupied with something else," she said. At the comment, Joey hummed pointedly, and June thought she saw Selena wave her off with an embarrassed giggle.

She distracted June with pronouns pins. Selena had a she/her one attached to her dress. June tried to keep her eyes on the pin and not to the dip where Selena's generous tits looked just heavenly.

The pins were magnetic and holographic, two things June loved and was grateful for. She loved the shirt she had on and didn't want to pin a needle through it no matter how harmless it might be.

"So, Selena's been your biggest fan for over a hundred years now. It's such a pleasure to meet you in real life. You have some of the best looks I've seen on that site," Joey said. She had a warm voice that spread all the way to June's dread-filled stomach.

She sat with June while Noor helped Selena put out some of the food they had brought. She could smell the pastries. Cheese. Yum.

"It's easy to stay away from using heels as contour brushes, believe me," she said. Joey cackled.

"Are you also into the whole modeling thing?"

"Oh, no. I like being behind my own camera, but I prefer applying the makeup than modeling it."

"It's a shame. I've been trying to convince Junie here to do a collaboration for ages," Selena said from the kitchen. With the open style of the place, her voice rang without it being overly loud.

June knew she was blushing. "Selena flatters me too much. I've told her this before, she's too beautiful to share a spotlight."

Joey's eyes widened, and she smirked at that.

"Ah, right," she murmured. June nodded and thanked god when the door rang, signaling the first of the small number of guests.

Once or twice, June fumbled with introduction but thankfully either Selena, Joey, or Noor helped her out. She was grateful for how quickly the couple adopted her as one of their own.

Selena was playing the perfect host. Ushering people to grab nonalcoholic refreshments and everyone seemed totally taken by how the place was set up. Something akin to pride bubbled in June's stomach. She could see how Selena was not just charming, she was genuine, and people gravitated towards her helplessly.

June had seen some TV episodes about baby showers, but Joey's little get-together was not like any of them at all. It didn't feel like a big deal. The parents-to-be seemed peaceful and calm while they held hands the whole time. They looked good together.

There was some ruckus over the gifts. A friend of Noor, named Amanda, gave Joey and Noor a coupon for babysitting which Joey kind of cried about. She probably hugged Amanda for close to five minutes.

When Noor opened June's gift, she cooed over the small shoes. "I am gonna hang this in the kiddo's bedroom."

June blushed and instead of murmuring anything embarrassing, she took a bite of her puff pastry. It was so good. There was a serving of pickles, which were so sour and delicious she kept sneaking bites from the plate whenever someone attempted to talk to her. Selena caught her avoiding socializing by humming over a piece and grinned. She got her out of the awkward one-sided conversation with a nod of her head. June apologized quickly and rushed over.

"Hey," she whispered.

Selena grinned, "Hi. Sorry you're having to stuff your face with pickles."

"Not at all. I love pickles," she said quietly. Selena grinned.

"Me too."

Oh, wow, can she get more appealing? She wondered as they had the weirdest conversation about pickles and how once Selena marathon-watched a TV show and had nothing but pickles and soda.

"It was the most surreal weekend of my life, but I'd do it again," she said wistfully. June recalled her own hazy weekends with Shelby, watching season after season of shows that were bad and good and entertaining beyond belief, eating pizza and shooing the cats away from their ice-cream.

As promised, the party was so intimate and comfortable to be at that June's anxiety didn't rear its ugly head. It helped too that she had a whole week of preparing herself mentally. Plus, that conversation she'd had with Selena centered her. It was nice to stand by the side as the attendees cracked up some anecdotes about their own kids, pets, and tiny relatives.

By eleven, the ambience turned mellower as people began to leave. It was the perfect timing for her to sneak out too. As if attuned to her, Selena met her eyes immediately when June looked for the brunette.

As if they gravitated to one another, or so June's affection addled brain supplied, they both met by a little area in the kitchen which was hidden from the living room and the few other guests. It felt intimate and all together good to be in proximity.

It wasn't as if June's mental problem shut down, it was more like it recognized that this wasn't a person who'd aggravate it.

If anything, Selena's smooth voice, humor, and endless consideration soothed June's anxiety.

"I'm so glad you could make it, Junie, here, I wrapped up some of the cupcakes for you." The food container made a sigh of relief bubble up inside her chest because she'd wanted a reason to be at Selena's again and she got it.

"I'll return this to you in like two days. I loved your cupcakes."

Selena waved a hand at her, dismissively but June repeated, "No, really, they're so good. Shelby will probably profess their love sometime soon."

"Well, if you get hungry for more, you're totally welcome to the eight hundred I've got left," Selena added with a wink.

June's chest felt lighter with giddiness.

They stood there, practically beaming at one another. June couldn't stop thinking of Selena's words from before. Getting to know each other. Wanting to be friends.

It was a big deal to June. As big of a deal as it was to Selena. She wanted unfiltered and genuine friendship. She wanted affection like that.

Their little bubble was burst when Joey came to find June.

"Junie—" Joey had adapted the nickname as well "—thank you so much for coming and for the micro-shoes! My baby will not wear them, but they'll cherish them forever," she said.

The hormones, love, and friendship made Joey very

loud with emotion. June rather liked seeing Joey's perfect exterior look turn disheveled with laughter and good fun. In the few hours she'd known her, June couldn't think of any other parent-to-be more deserving of joy.

Joey also fell into June's arms in a hug, as much as a six feet woman could fall into June's arms.

June, who was usually not that great about unexpected hugs, simply wrapped her arms around her and patted her back.

Noor came to the rescue, whisking her beautiful wife with an apologetic smile. "So sorry, she's usually all about asking permission before physical contact but–"

"No need! It's okay!" June interrupted. She waved at Joey, who waved back and sheepishly hid her face in her spouse's neck. She seemed to be coming off the emotional high.

Selena was watching all of it unwrap with an indecipherable smile.

"What's that for?"

"What?"

"That secret smile."

"Oh, that's nothing," she dragged the syllables.

June didn't believe her at all but at that point, she couldn't help herself from smiling back. Her face probably got the most exercise in smiling the past four hours than it ever did the past three months.

They shuffled over to the entrance together and Selena got June her jacket from the little closet by the door.

June kneeled down to tie her shoelaces and when she straightened up, Selena stood a bit closer. She could see a fleck of sparkle —probably from the cupcakes— on the side of her lips, and June cursed her romance inflated brain for making her imagine wiping it off with her fingertip.

They stood there, June waiting for something she couldn't quite put a finger on and Selena looking a bit worn out but still as lovely as ever.

"Come here," Selena said, her voice low, as she opened her arms. June walked into the hug, glad for Selena's forwardness. She wanted to go wherever Selena told her to go. And if it was into her vanilla and almond smelling arms, soft plush chest, then she'd be more than happy to.

She wrapped her arms around Selena. They were the same height and it put her face against Selena's head. She wondered if she could possibly pay Selena for her hugs.

A deep sigh emitted from her chest and wow, thank god Selena didn't comment on it because June was pretty sure she was mortified for a second there.

But the sigh, involuntary and totally necessary, made Selena squeeze her tighter, which was the closest thing June would ever come to experiencing a moment of absolute peace and heavenly warmth.

She drove back home with a dorky smile on her face that she worried would stop her cats from recognizing her.

☼

CHAPTER THREE

June: She's just... sunshine reincarnated into a woman. And what a woman she is. She's like sweet, considerate and a FUCKIN' BAKER. She smells SO GOOD.

Shelby: Just marry her, June. I'm delirious with fever but I support it.

June: I might just take your advice.

June: Do you think she'll judge me for having my cats sleep with me?

June: By the way, are you sure you don't need me to come over to nurse you to health?

Shelby: Uh, she better not. Judging you is my job.

Shelby: And no. My mom already sent me thirteen home remedies that use up some sort of herb. She also popped by my place, freaking out my roommate at 10 PM.

June: Oh, Shelbz, you're a charmer how are you still single?

Shelby: Because I'm unfortunately too good for everyone.

June: But!!!! I believe!!! U are 2 soft 2 b single

Shelby: Tumblr 2010 called, it wants its bad texting style back.

June: [tongue out emoji]

Shelby: Anyway, why are we talking about me?

Shelby: Me = sad and lonely.

Shelby: Let's talk about the future Mrs. Bana.

June: [blushing emojis] Have I told you that she like has like... the magical ability to destroy me with a smile? I barely stop my brain from short circuiting because like she's always smiling. What. An. Angel.

Shelby: You're so gone! I'm so happy for you.

June: Urggghhhh this is so ugh!!!!

Shelby: Words. Use them.

June: Sorry. Can't. Selena Clarke Stole My Words.

Shelby: Pfft. Anyway, gotta go, FK is hounding me today because I took (1) day off.

June: Fuck Karen!

J une sent one last text before she had to tuck her phone away. Her next client was ready, and June flexed her fingers for another two hours of applying makeup on young prom goers. Business was good for a freelance makeup artist in LA.

June found that the monotony of routine fit her so well with her job. Sure, she had a packed schedule, and ended up working for hours into the night sometimes, but she also had a great deal of endorsements thanks to her online presence.

Work had a complex space in June's life that terrified her when she thought of it too much.

But most of the time, the career she pursued always reminded her that she was in a semblance space of happiness.

Nine months ago, after Selena and June's first offline introduction, they had started, what June considered, a good online friendship. Selena commented on June's looks and June liked Selena's posts first, almost always.

She'd gotten that direct message from Selena on a day where she needed something to get her blood pumping. When she agreed to doing Selena's makeup for a shoot when the makeup artist had to back out, June had gotten so nervous she cried herself to sleep the night before.

The location had been quite close though and with every mile, June's brain had calmed down, her *Hamilton* soundtrack had blared at a respectably good volume so that she didn't bother other people but still didn't hear herself singing along to *Satisfied*.

Thanks to an overzealous assistant, June had soon found her makeup station and with her usual routine all mapped out, she organized her things. She had met Selena in the flesh soon after.

The model had walked in wearing a floral romper with spaghetti straps that left so much of her brown skin to bask in the sun. Selena's hand was so soft and warm when June shook it. Not warm as in sweaty. It was as if it had stored sun inside of it. As if Selena herself was the sun. With stars in her eyes, June couldn't do much besides stare that first time Selena gave her a full smile.

June wasn't immune to charming people and that counted Selena with her easy smile and nosiness about June's makeup technique. Her questions surprisingly hadn't made June bunch her shoulders up into a knot of insecurity. Rather, they had made her smile and explain in many more words than she'd normally use.

"I admit. I followed you because of your tattoo picture." Ah. The cats tattoo picture that June had splurged on and that went viral. Everyone seemed to have seen it. A tiny part of June liked the attention. It was a tattoo of her babies, Lemon and Mint, and she was especially proud of how it looked.

"Thanks. I... uh followed you four years ago," she had mumbled as she highlighted the bridge of Selena's nose.

Selena's eyes had widened, the brown accentuated with

the shade of shimmering peach June had used generously. "Wait, I wasn't even that known four years ago."

June had shrugged.

"Oh, my god, you're like my first legit fan, aren't you?"

"Maybe so," June had blushed and said. Selena chuckled a bit.

"You're so cool. I don't know how I'm keeping my shit together," Selena murmured.

June scoffed. Her? Cool? Try anxious. Yet her faced burned. God, she was blushing so much.

"No, you are," Selena had replied with a grin. "Your Instagram account basically has nothing on it that isn't about makeup. People barely even know how old you are." With a gasp shed added, "Are you a vampire?"

June couldn't help herself, she'd laughed. "No. Just boring. I'm twenty-five."

Selena grinned. "And how long have you been twenty-five?"

After a long-ish pause, June whispered, "A while." Selena practically burst into giggles. Nothing like a Twilight reference to bring together two gals. June gave her a wink.

"As I said, cool as fuck."

No matter how many times Selena tried to relax her face, it remained in a soft smile.

June hadn't thought of her life as interesting enough as for someone like Selena to be curious about it.

The added weight of being somewhat well known on Instagram spooked her. She had always maintained a low-key presence online. Her Facebook had just gotten connected to her Instagram three months prior. Every time she hit a new thousand followers she felt an awe of not deserving any of the positive comments.

Selena's comment about her "coolness" had stayed with her. Through the rest of the makeup, the shoot, the tiny here and there touch-ups, and even the next day when she edited a picture she took of Selena behind the scenes.

She'd hesitated a couple of times over sending it to her but when she opened the direct messages between them and saw Selena's small icon of her, smiling, with her head thrown back? She said fuck it and sent it.

> **BANAJOON** sent a picture
> Is it okay to post this?

SelenaSClarke
YES [sparkle emoji]
i look so good!!!!

When June posted the picture, it was accompanied by a caption that had a little more commentary than her usual usage of an emoji or a line from a book she had read and the list of products she'd used in the case of a makeup post. That one was accompanied by, "Sunshine, move on, @SelenaSClarke is here. It was a blessing. [sparkle emoji x1]"

The first comment and like were, unsurprisingly, Selena's.

SelenaSClarke: [blushing   emoji]   [sunshine emoji] #teamjune

---

Did she like that a potential crush –fuck potential, definite was more like it– had an inside joke with her? Fuck yeah, she did.

And so on, every new post Selena had put on June's feed called out to her. Or, the push notification did. Either way, she found that her mind always supplied her with something to say. She kind of felt more comfortable as a commentator.

And in real life, it was back to the easy rapport whenever June had Selena sitting in her makeup chair.

So, for nine months, June convinced herself that no way did Selena see her comments when she got hundreds per day. But that obviously was untrue. Selena basically confirmed that the fluttering excitement June had was mutual. The comfort of knowing that Selena wanted to know more about her made all sorts of delightful noises happen inside June's head.

Did it worry her that it might become something romantic? It did. It scared her shitless.

She wasn't much of a dater. The last relationship she had, she was eighteen and it was just emotionally taxing as well as nerve-racking. Also, coming into terms of her newly-found sexuality was not easy. June might have been "cool as fuck" but she was aware of her own expectations in a relationship.

Some part of her always yearned for something that enveloped her not in a sense of passion but a calm care. She wanted someone she could rely on to not always expect her to perform. Someone who saw how quiet she was and respected it. Not that her ex-boyfriend didn't. It was the expectation the relationship put on her that broke her a little.

Being long distance and anxious didn't mesh well at all. Days would pass without her texting back or initiating a conversation and it'd just hurt Miles. And it hurt their friendship. It wasn't good for them. Above all, June cherished friendships. Hence, she broke things off and the two maintained a comfortable friendship that had more of them catching up every couple of months and texting deep into the night when something unique to the months long of interests they developed together popped up.

But being around Selena, basking in the glory of her presence, and having that sense that she was nothing but herself with her made things seem kind of easy. Handleable.

SelenaSClarke

hey junie!!!!

June's eyes were bleary, one glamorous look following another did that to her. Her back cracked and her fingers were smudged with glitter, eyelash glue, and dark stuff that'll take a hot shower to get from under her nails. But the second she heard her phone's special notification she'd set for Selena, she perked up.

Much like her comments, texts with Selena felt easy since there was zero chance of Selena seeing her reactions. Which often was her blushing and getting tongue-tied.

SelenaSClarke

wanna hang out sometime soon?

soon being tomorrow??

sometime around three thirty

pm

BANAJOON

Yes, sure.

Is this for a work thing?

SelenaSClarke

oh no. i was on ur page and got overwhelmed, like usual,
and thought i'd ask u out

BANAJOON

Overwhelmed?

SelenaSClarke

oh!!! yeah! always it's a perpetual state of mind for me... esp
around cute makeup artists...

artist...

singular...

"Oh, fuck, she's so adorable," June whispered to herself.
She sat down and cracked her worn out fingers. Which,
ouch, she shouldn't have.

BANAJOON

Where do you have in mind?

SelenaSClarke

there's this really cute dessert place
i could pick you up!!!

BANAJOON

You drive?

SelenaSClarke

not a lot but when it matters

BANAJOON

You just totally made me smile even in my state of
destroyed-post-prom appointments.

SelenaSClarke

you had prom apps!!!! how did they go??? i wish someone as
good as you did my prom makeup

BANAJOON

Who did your prom makeup? Also, are there any pics?

SelenaSClarke

i did my makeup lollll which is why i looked average af
also,,,, maybe there are. i'll show you some pics tomorrow (if
i rmb)

BANAJOON

Tease. Also, no way in heck would you ever look 'average.'
It's blasphemous of you to even say that.

SelenaSClarke

[blushing emojis x10]
you're so nice.

BANAJOON

Again, I'm just being honest.

SelenaSClarke

well...... i like all Junes, honest June, complimentary June.....

that sounds like u come with like.... a hotel room...
and im totes not thinking of u in a hotel room
nope
not at allllll

BANAJOON
[heart emojis x20]
You're such a mess.

SelenaSClarke
your kind of mess?

BANAJOON
Totally.

CHAPTER FOUR

The weather had surprisingly warmed over the past week, probably due to global warming, so June felt comfortable showing a little skin.

She smoothed down the shirt she specifically ironed for her date. Which was totally a friendly date. Her getting to know a friend with potential dating in the future date. Either way, she was so excited she could barely keep the goofy smile off her face.

When Shelby's FaceTime call came at two p.m., they joked nonstop about it. June couldn't even snark back she just was goofily smiling all day long. Even her cats looked weary of her good mood.

She stood before her floor length mirror, French tucked her shirt into her shorts; which were modest and fell to her knees and were black. She liked the tucked look but in an act of truly betraying Tan France she undid it. Tying the ends around her stomach revealed a bit of belly just between where the high-waist of the shorts started, and the t-shirt ended. It gave her a boost of confidence she hadn't known she needed.

She sent a picture, or maybe a hundred, to Shelby.

Shelby: hawt hawt hawt

The shirt was simple in the front but the whole back was sheer and allowed her to show off her orange lacy bra (which she spent fifty dollars on!).

Her phone rang for a couple of seconds, Marina singing something about having a figure like a pin-up, a figure like a doll. Then it stopped. *She's outside* yelled her insides, rather calmly. June checked that she carried her keys, her phone, and her wallet one last time and pet her boys.

Her sandals, shiny and pink, made a satisfying smack against the asphalt outside her apartment building. She saw that Selena had parallel parked perfectly. June couldn't believe that her crush is a gay who could drive. Oh wow, her crush got even bigger.

Selena lowered the window and said, "Get in, sweetie, it's time for dessert."

June smiled and shook her head at the mixture of references. She didn't even know where to start with deconstructing that.

Once she buckled in, she turned to give Selena a hello.

"Holy biscuit. You look so lovely I genuinely think I have heart-eyes right now," Selena's words rushed out.

June felt the telltale of a blush creeping up her neck and she grinned. Smiling was just so much fun around her.

Selena grinned back. Her mouth was pink in the center and glossy. Gosh, darn it, she looked uber-soft.

Her hair was in curls, framing her cheeks. She had on an off-shoulder dress which was bombarded with flowers big and small. June's eyes trailed the buttons in the front to the very end where the dress ended between Selena's legs. When she looked up, Selena gave her a knowing look.

Damn, was that too much? Am I weirding her out? She wanted to panic but Selena didn't seem bothered, she just threw a wink at her and put the car in drive.

The drive was quick but comfortable. They listened to Troy Sivan and June stole glances at Selena's profile as she mouthed the lyrics. In the distance, the sun began to set, casting a warm orange and pink glow in the car. June's heart caught in the way Selena's eyes turned a couple shades lighter, the way the gloss on her mouth looked more appetizing than any dessert June could ever put in her mouth.

"So, did you have a good week?" June tried at conversation. She wasn't great with small talk but because it made Selena smile, she was going to do her best.

"Oh, yeah! Remember that trip I told you about?"

"To your mom's?"

"Yeah! Well, I had to stay there for only a couple of days, but it was so good to see her and everyone else." Selena's voice was filled with longing.

"Do you miss her often?"

"I mean, I can't miss her. We text and FaceTime a lot. Even on the plane there, I was texting my sisters and asking who was gonna have the honor of picking me up." She laughed.

"It didn't feel like a homecoming because I've always felt at home, I suppose."

June nodded absently. She didn't feel exactly the same because although her mom lived twenty minutes away, they mostly texted. Not in a bad way. Just in a *we're both busy and are bad with communication* way.

"What about you? Do you see your mom often?"

It was as if she'd read her mind. June shook her head.

"She drops by sometimes with groceries whenever I go more than three days without sending her a picture of the cats, so, yeah."

"That's so nice. That she takes care of you."

"Oh yeah, she's very... mother hen. I don't know if it's her wanting to control everything or because she just cares so much. She even hosts dinners for the booksellers in Bastoog on special occasions."

Selena giggled. "I can totally relate to that. I'm a bit of a fussy person too. But ever since I got a full-time job being a model I've eased up."

"Hmmm, maybe I should get my mom modeling. That'll get her to stop texting me about her lunches."

"Hey, that actually sounds really good. Does she cook a lot of Middle Eastern food?"

June gave Selena a teasing look.

"You're gonna have to be a *little* more specific there. Middle Eastern food is... very diverse."

"Oh! Sorry! I mean, she is considered Khaleeji right?" She gave June an apologetic look. June waved her off.

"Yep! And she does make a lot of Khaleeji food. Mostly rice dishes that always put me in a food coma."

"Again, sounds really good to me," Selena murmured. "Oh, here we are!"

Selena slowed down at a gated parking lot. She reached out for a ticket and grinned as she maneuvered into a park. The sun was still doing its peachy pink magic when Selena turned the engine off.

June's mind brought up the thought of all those movies she watched with Shelby, where a couple in similar situations always ended up making out and fogging up the windows.

"Let's go," Selena said.

June, again, left her clichéd thoughts behind. There was no space for absentmindedness.

The place was called Graham's Delicacies and it was everything in a perfect aesthetic board. It had soft pink wallpaper, set off with creamy chairs that looked comfy, tables that were the perfect height, and lighting that allowed enough sunlight in to give the gold detail a sparkle.

June was enchanted as fuck.

It also helped that the music they played was a soft R&B playlist that didn't clash with the overall theme of soft pinks and golds of the lettering on the glass window. It was perfectly balanced between soothing and comfortable.

It didn't feel like the six other people, sitting in tables dispersed around the place, would be listening in to their conversation.

As a matter of fact, only one person looked up at their entrance but looked away quickly enough.

"Wanna get a booth? Or is a regular table fine?" Selena wiggled her brows. It was oddly cute of her to do.

June shrugged. She really didn't mind either.

Selena led them to a combination of both. The corner table was away from everyone else and small enough that June's legs brushed Selena's. God bless this table.

Swiftly, they were given a menu by a perky staff with a name tag that said Jen. Their red hair was a perfect halo around their head as they spoke about the special cakes specific to that day.

"Thank you so much," Selena said enthusiastically. Her mouth was its usual wide smile. June buried her face in her menu. She was so consumed by the warm feelings in her stomach. She knew they must have been showing on her face.

"Everything looks good, yeah? I've wanted to come here

for months," Selena murmured. June looked up.

"Oh, you've never been here?" June fiddled with the center piece.

Selena shook her head. It tousled her curls.

"Why not?" Something in the way Selena avoided eye-contact made June extremely nosy.

"I... uh, wanted to come with you," Selena whispered.

June's brain turned to sludge as it tried to process the information.

"Wait. Didn't you say you've wanted to come here for months?" She leaned close and watched Selena's hands reach for a napkin. She began to shred it.

"Yeah..." she trailed off. "I wanted to save the visit for someone special. Guess I always planned to come here with you."

June was dumbfounded.

Months. Selena might have been carrying a torch for June since... they first met. She didn't know what to do with the information. And even if she did, she was tongue-tied. She just nodded.

For a couple of seconds, they silently perused the soft pink lamented menu. It was short and as Selena said, everything looked yummy, but June's eyes couldn't decide on anything.

"Okay, hold up, so does this mean this is a date?" she blurted.

Selena looked up with a start but nodded. Assuredly. No second of hesitation. No chance to misunderstand.

"Oh. Okay." June's eyes fell back to her menu and she might had had a true moment of true joy where inner-June pumped her fists and shouted.

Her head a bit clearer, June's eyes gravitated towards the saffron cake. She wondered if it was as good as the ones she used to eat from the shop around the corner from her childhood apartment.

"What about the saffron cake?" she asked.

Selena hummed. Her eyebrows furrowed, deep in thought. Very reasonable. Cake was a *serious* matter.

"I think I'll go with the Japanese pancakes," Selena decided.

"Oh, have you ever had those before?"

"Nope. They sound delish though."

Through ordering their desserts, June's head, while still rejoicing over the date bit, was still preoccupied with how the date fit with the fact that Selena might have had feelings for her. She kind of felt that fluttery thing she associated with crushes and it made her look solidly at the table.

"What's wrong?" Selena asked.

June took a deep breath. She was about to do it. She was going to ask directly.

"Do you have feelings for me? Romantic feelings?"

Selena's eyes widened a bit and the curve to her lips got wider. June noticed how her hand went to the base of her neck. She rubbed the thin chain of her necklace.

"Is it bad?"

"No, not at all, but I'm trying to convince my brain this just happened."

"Oh, yeah sure. Yes," Selena said with a smile. "I like you. Romantic stylez—"

"With a z," June joined in to complete. She laughed. Wow.

Was that what a miracle felt like? She had read a lot of stories when she was young about prophets doing miracles, but while a big part of June yelled that this wasn't the same, a bigger part wasn't convinced. *I don't know*, she thought, *it does kind of feel earth shattering and wonderful all at once.*

Selena's hand lowered from her necklace and June's eyes were practically glued on her movements. She squirmed a little and June realized it. Selena just admitted something so huge and June had said nothing in reply except for a Brooklyn Nine-Nine reference.

"I do too— I mean, I like you too. Romantic stylez with a z and all," June said surely.

The weight on her chest didn't feel overwhelming, not with the dying sun seeming to shine a little bit brighter with Selena's full-blown grin. Her mouth was so lovely. So were her eyes. The roundness of her cheeks. The way her fingers looked when she held anything. The shake of her thighs when she danced. June liked everything about Selena.

"It's kind of scary, isn't it?" Selena asked in a murmur. June nervously tapped her feet.

"Terrifying."

"But not in a bad way. It's like I opened a door to a whole new thing in my chest and I'm, like, excited to go through," Selena explained. "No pressure," she hurried to add.

June laughed at that last bit.

"Somehow, my anxiety is not getting the memo to freak the fuck out," she replied.

Their conversation was interrupted by their cakes arriving. The Japanese pancakes were so surprisingly small and soft that when June bit into the piled-up mix on her fork, she hummed in pleasure. She fed Selena a bite to share in the experience. Selena gave a satisfying groan.

June could have written poetry about how the mesh of cream and caramel complimented the berries. And she told Selena. Selena grinned and agreed.

"It's so soft I feel like I need to protect it," she added. June smiled.

They also shared her saffron cake with June sharing the stories of her mom failing a lot in trying to make it. How it was a treat so associated with home, with its cramped spaces and the sound of Persian words flowing over her head from her mom and dad, that every bite into the softness brought her back in time.

Selena shared her own wild stories of being the youngest of four girls. "Wow." June looked at her in wonder. It somehow turned into Selena showing her all the scars she accumulated playing rough with her sisters.

"I have so many siblings and nephews and nieces that they make up my fan base, basically," she joked. Then scoffed at herself. "Fan base. That's the most ridiculous thing ever."

"How come? You're an icon." June wasn't even sarcastic.

"I've never been the kind of gal who had 'fans,' and even uttering the words makes me disbelieve it all. It seems like the kind of prank some vicious asshole would pull on me," she murmured between bites from the saffron cake. She also waved her fork around as she spoke.

Her free hand rested on the table, so June took a breath and reached to hold it.

Unfortunately, that startled Selena and she jerked, knocking her juice glass. It spilled over her lap and the chill must have made her yelp. June was caught both in shock and the urge to laugh but she did neither. She began to apologize. Almost too much. Noticing June's flailing in trying to soak up the juice from Selena's dress and the table, their waiter whisked in to rescue them by getting extra napkins.

"Oh god, I'm so sorry."

Selena laughed. "It's okay. I'm just–I wasn't prepared, I guess."

June's stomach plummeted. She didn't know what to do or say, she just watched Selena try and pat her lap dry.

Selena looked up from the mess and caught June's crest-fallen face.

"June, it isn't you. I was surprised. I didn't think you would try to hold my hand." Something sounded a bit hesitant in Selena's voice.

June wanted to ignore it and just move on from what was beginning to seem like a failing first date. But. No. She wouldn't. She won't let anxiety take this one good thing from her.

"I'm sorry but why didn't you think I would try and hold your hand?"

At this, Selena's eyes softened, and it wasn't what June expected. She thought Selena might try and evade the assumption. June knew people noticed her lack of warmth. She dealt with touching people daily at her job, but plenty noticed when she would push away from a hug and when she'd not get super close to take selfies.

"June, I want you to be comfortable with me. I don't want you to think that you have to push yourself out of your comfort zone just because I asked you out on a date." June's heart settled in her chest. It'd been banging so hard.

Somehow, the words made tears spring up in her eyes.

Selena *got* it. She got June's wariness of touch. She got how uncomfortable it made her to be touched without warning. Sure, Joey hugged her, but it was a spur of the moment action that June could forgive.

Selena somehow saw her hesitance. She saw how every little thing affected her.

Was it selfish to enjoy someone's attention to detail? To her details? Maybe. She didn't mind being selfish in this case.

"Thank you," she managed to choke out.

"You don't have to thank me for respecting your personal boundaries. I respect you and your autonomy, Junie."

Selena gave her the same soft look that June couldn't decipher. Was she pitying her? No, she wouldn't. Selena just said she respected her. She shook her head a bit. She felt all kinds of messy inside, so she focused on what was on Selena's lap.

"We should get your dress dry; it can't be comfortable." She knew she changed the subject, but Selena's kind face smiled, and she felt okay.

"This isn't drying anytime soon and it's gonna ruin the white flowers if I don't get it cleaned asap," Selena said with a tiny huff. Her dress didn't look wet thanks to the pattern, but she was right. The tiny white flowers clustered in one area looked orange. Also, it must had been quite uncomfortable to sit with a tacky cold dress on.

"We can go back to my place. I ca--" She cleared her throat and tried again. "I can wash it for you." She wasn't sure she liked her own tone. She sounded so small and hesitant. But Selena perked up.

"You can do laundry?" Selena asked disbelievingly.

"Yeah. I mean, can't live alone for as long as I have without learning to," she said in a way of explanation.

"You're so grown up. Would it be okay? I really love this dress and it'll stain if I leave it." Selena bit into her lip.

"Yeah, it's the least I can do. Also, it's no hassle. There are some machines in my buildings' basement. Would you mind staying at my place in the meantime?"

June breathed a sigh of relief at Selena's immediate nod.

※☼※

CHAPTER FIVE

June didn't have the time to worry over the plain lobby or the cracked staircase. She was distracted by Selena behind her.

Her presence made heat rise in June's cheeks. Selena's heels were surprisingly silent and made June aware of every inhale she took. She unlocked her door which prompted Mint to come and observe. She didn't have much of an entryway, just a small area to shelve her everyday shoes. She removed her shoes and Selena followed suit.

"Sorry I don't really have slippers."

"It's okay!"

Mint watched the two of them with a tilt to his incredibly adorable head, his green eyes shadowed by the dim light. June leaned down to grab him. She ignored the possibility of getting her shirt covered in fur, she needed the physical closeness of her baby right then.

"Your place is so homey," Selena said. June thanked her. She wasn't wrong.

The place was small and expensive but that was the rate everywhere. June had a well sized living room with a couch her mom donated to make her feel at home, as well as some book shelves she got cheap from an acquaintance who moved out of state. There was a kitchen, a bathroom, and her bedroom.

The last consisted of a low bed. The bed she would never regret, ever. She'd splurged on it from her first and last paycheck at Sephora six months ago, which she had to quit the job due to anxiety issues. Plus, she had a little corner where she shot her quick Instagram videos and pictures.

She tried to see the place from Selena's eyes but couldn't. It was her home. Her little haven. She just hoped she didn't forget any stray snack wrappers from her last episode. She got snacky when she was depressed.

After two minutes of them standing in the living room, with Selena looking over the bookshelves and June trying to keep Mint happy in her arms, Lemon slowly walked into the room as if he owned it. The feline had a look on his face that said he was just woken up and he did not appreciate it at all. It was the one of his two moods. Okay, that wasn't fair, but June loved how perpetually grumpy he looked.

"Okay, sir," Selena murmured, and June laughed. Selena sat on the couch and patted her lap. She grimaced, remembering the state of her dress.

"Oh yeah, follow me and I'll get you something to change into," June said as she put down Mint and rushed to her bedroom.

Once they were inside, the situation caught up with her. She was in her bedroom with the girl occupying an embarrassingly large portion of her thought. Having a one-track mind did come in handy then and it helped June stay focused. June headed directly to her wardrobe and rummaged through her comfortable stuff.

She thanked God both she and Selena had similarly

shaped wide hips and cushy thighs. She got a pair of sweat-pants from her hefty collection and a worn but loved Captain America T-shirt. Selena eyed the outfit with a twist to her mouth.

"Is anything wrong?" June turned a critical eye to the clothes in her hands.

"No, no. I'm just—it's nice. To be able to borrow some-one's clothes without worrying about the fit." She thumbed the t-shirt almost lovingly. June felt a warmth, not like the one from embarrassment, rise in her chest. She shrugged and took a swift exit.

June felt how momentous it was to her too. She'd always been conscious of her size around thin people, but not once had she felt othered by Selena's body.

Two minutes later, Selena handed her the dress through the door's opening.

"I'm gonna go pop this in a machine downstairs and come back." Selena nodded. Lemon and Mint eyed her with twin looks of curiosity.

Ignoring their looks, June hurried and grabbed her personal basket with some detergent and fabric softener. Her trip to the basement was quick. The place was well lit and empty. The building might had been worn out, but it had honest people running it.

Once June made sure she had a nice cycle going, she went back up. She found Selena in the kitchen, fiddling with a kettle.

"Here, let me help," she murmured. It was a small kitchen. She was hyperaware of how close they huddled. Selena looked absolutely adorable with her feet bare and her mossy green painted nails wiggling. As expected, when June stole glances at Selena, the t-shirt and the sweatpants fit perfectly.

While June definitely felt bad about their date getting cut short, she didn't mind the quiet companionship they shared as June fixed their tea as they liked. As Selena added some sugar and a tiny speck of milk to her tea, she must have noticed Lemon and Mint being grade A stalkers.

She nodded to the audience of two furries watching them. "Are they always this observant?"

"Not all the time but mostly. They're curious about guests. I don't get a lot since I work part-time at this local salon." June took a sip of tea and winced. It was hot.

"Oh, yeah? That's where you take your client's pictures?"

"Yep. This place is too small, and I like keeping my makeup supplies locked up in the salon. Also, I've been working there for quite some time and it's just been the best for my anxiety."

"How so? If you don't mind me asking." Selena nudged her feet with hers and gave her a tiny smile.

"That's fine. It's just that, working a nine to five shift never worked for me. Anxiety keeps me up till morning sometimes and bailing on shifts because I didn't get any sleep did not work at all," she said.

They sat down with their mugs on the couch. Tiny as it was, it left no space between them. Their thighs brushed, and June appreciated the way their bodies seemed to fit together. Soft on soft.

"Does it happen often? The anxiety at night?" Selena faced her and leaned forward as she asked. Her face relaxed, but her tone concerned.

"Kind of? I was always terrified of messing up. I—" she paused. Her chest was getting tight. She swallowed back.

Selena got even closer and pressed her shoulder against June's. "It's okay, you don't have to talk about it. I'm glad you're doing something more suitable to your mental health now."

June smiled wearily. She still felt that shock of uselessness that depression convinced her of. She couldn't get the worry of never being financially stable out from under her skin. It lived and festered. Every morning became a nightmare for her.

She took a sip from her tea and winced for a different reason. "Fuck. I shouldn't be drinking caffeine this late."

Selena started. "Gimmie it. Caffeine doesn't hurt me that much. I can handle it."

June watched her slurp from her drink after a couple of blown breaths.

"Ugh, you put too much milk in your tea, babe," Selena whined. June's heart stuttered at the term of endearment.

"You're so—" she waved her hands. Selena arched an eyebrow at that.

"I don't know how to finish that. I don't think I've ever met anyone who was this kind to me since Shelby." She fiddled with her fingers. She still had on her date outfit which made her feel a bit ridiculous. Her mutual crush—the words were as mind boggling as when she'd first heard Selena's confession—sat next to her and June couldn't even hold eye contact.

"You deserve kindness, Junie." Selena put down the tea cup, nearly empty, and gave June's knee a supportive squeeze.

The sound of June's alarm sounded off. Thirty minutes had passed by so quickly and she hadn't even noticed.

"I gotta go get your dress. Would it be okay to leave you with the cats? They'll just try to sit on your lap and get petted." She nodded her head at Mint and Lemon perched by their feet. Selena smiled at the gremlins.

"Yeah, sure. Thanks again. Means a lot."

"Again, kind of my fault, so," she trailed off. She quickly put on her comfy flats and headed to the laundry room.

THE DRESS CLEAN AND SPOTLESS IN HER HAND, JUNE took the stairs to her apartment with a little jump in her step. Selena was still on the couch, surrounded by throw pillows and June's fur babies. Selena had one hand behind Mint's ear, stroking rhythmically as she scratched under Lemon's chin.

"You look cozy," June said. She had a hanger she used to dry her clothes and that's where she hung Selena's dress. Unfortunately, it was dark outside so there wouldn't be any sun to help quicken the drying process. *Or, was it fortunately?* June's brain supplied.

"They warmed up to me so fast. I kind of feel special." Selena's hands must have been cramping but she didn't seem bothered.

She scooted, and June sat relatively closer than she planned. The couch was small, and the dip in the cushion let her right thigh touch Selena's left even more solidly than before. Her eyes were drawn to that area. Warmth beyond belief emitted there. It was comfortable as heck and she signaled Mint to come to her. Like the good boy he was, he abandoned Selena's lap and stepped over to June's, his paws painful but not unbearably so. She was used to his weight. Could even distinguish which one climbed on her back when she indulged in her afternoon naps.

"So, is it just you and Mint and Lemon?"

"Pretty much. My best friend Shelby visits sometimes and is my unofficial assistant. They just make sure I'm not in bed an hour before a big appointment. I pay them with makeup looks when they can't be bothered to do it themself."

"You seem close. Have you known them for long?"

"We met on Twitter. Ranting about this show that kept queerbaiting its viewers, you know, like all the damn shows," she murmured.

Mint settled down in her lap after a rigorous kneading and let her rub him as much as she liked. It calmed her down and made her remember that she would have liked to change out of her clothes.

That thought reminded her of Selena in her t-shirt. June leaned back and looked over Selena. She was taking pictures of Lemon's head which rested on her thigh.

"He looks very grumpy but is a big softie," Selena said when she noticed June's eyes on her. She had a lovely flush that made her skin glow. She had wiped her lipstick which left her mouth looking somewhat even more striking than before. June looked away but whoops, Selena noticed her eyes on her mouth. The quiet apartment, except for the soft purring of both felines, didn't feel stifling. June usually couldn't sit without music playing whether she worked on a look or a video or whatever. She hated the quiet. But this quiet, filled with nearly palpable static between her and Selena, was good. Selena leaned back too. Her cheek rested on the back of the couch.

"Not bad for a first date, huh?" Selena asked softly. June blinked. She hadn't even thought it had counted to sit on her couch staring at one another to be part of the date.

She said as much to Selena.

"I personally think this is one of the best parts of today, though," Selena said. She leaned infinitesimally closer but June, hyper aware as usual, couldn't help herself from taking a deeper breath than usual. She wanted the physical contact. But she wasn't sure how to initiate. If she even wanted to initiate it. Sometimes she liked being the one giving the yes rather than the one asking. It messed with her head too much to think of being rejected.

As if reading her mind, Selena's free hand inched closer. With a look to June's own free hand, the realization struck. Their date was about to get seventy percent more heart stopping. She inched her pinky until it touched Selena's.

Romance novels, which June gobbled up in her free time, all told June she should feel electrocuted. It sounded scary and kind of bad. It made her so conscious of her lack of lightning with Miles. Every time his slender fingers would wrap around her ink stained ones –she always bought cheap pens that bled all over her fingers—June had been distracted focusing on what she should have been feeling and hadn't appreciated the comfort in having his cool hand around her warm one.

But in that second, when Selena's pinky wrapped around hers in response, June's mind didn't stray. If anything, she felt immersed in the moment. There was no lightning, thank god, she was extremely terrified of lightning, but there was warmth. The smooth pads felt squishy. Like touching Lemon or Mint's paws.

And when Selena wrapped June's hand in hers completely, the palm on palm action felt like a tiny sparkler.

Something she could handle.

Something she could welcome.

She'd touched Selena's hand before, when applying makeup for intricate shoots. But this felt different.

Especially with Selena biting her plush lower lip. Her lashes fluttered as she looked up to June. June wondered what Selena saw in her. If she saw the flaws June saw. If she saw the light June tried to remind herself existed within herself.

"Do you want to watch something?" June asked mutedly. An air of tension surrounded them. She didn't want to disturb it. Selena's mouth quirked at the question.

"Sure. What do you have in mind?"

"I have Avatar the Last Airbender," June suggested. Selena's eyebrow rose.

"Oh, yay, let's watch that."

With reluctance, June pulled her hand from Selena's and had to put Mint down, which didn't appeal to him at all. "I'll be a minute; I'll grab my laptop and change."

"I'll be here," Selena said.

With those words, June's anxiety took a permanent seat in the back of her head for the remainder of the night. She just busied herself thinking of the warm and comfortable hand holding. How no expectation or pressure of going further made it so simple and yet so exhilarating. The comfort of being snuggled with two cats on-and-off sitting between them, then going off to play loudly in June's room permeated the mood.

They had watched four episodes of the show, Selena oohed at the impressive bits and giggled at the jokes Sokka pummeled the audience with.

By the end of that episode, Selena yawned, which sounded like she'd tried to force it down.

"You're tired," June stated the obvious.

Selena smiled. "A little. Yeah."

"You should get home then, so you won't be too tired to drive." She looked at their conjoined hands, her thumb rubbed circled on Selena's skin.

"You're so right, girlfriend," she murmured, and June's eyes flew to hers.

"So, we're using that? We're girlfriends?" she asked hopefully.

Selena bit her lip and grinned. "Yeah, definitely. We're girlfriends with labels and everything."

"Wow," June said and felt immediately silly. Selena grinned though and lifted their hands to plant a kiss against the back of June's palm.

"I presume you're okay with that, right?"

June nodded.

"More than okay."

"Okayest."

June gave a tired laugh and poked Selena's cheek, right where her dimple formed.

"Would you be okayest with me telling people?"

June presumed Selena meant her thousands of followers. For a second there, June had to push her mind out of the comfort zone they'd cocooned themselves in and consider what it'd mean for them to be that public that soon.

The anxiety rushed into her stomach and left her breathless.

"Uh, not really," she choked out. She took a deeper breath and tried to erase any worries Selena might get. "It's kind of a big deal since I'm not even *that* open about my private life on my account. So, I don't want to open such a big part of my life to people."

Selena's face closed a bit, but she nodded with her eyes glued to their hands in her lap.

"Selena, it's not me not trusting you or not wanting to rush in because I don't believe in us working out. I just love my privacy a little too much."

Selena looked up and nodded. "I understand. I'm sorry if my question caused you any anxiety. I totally get it. And I would do my best to protect your privacy."

June squeezed her hand and pulled her close. That earned her a kiss on the cheek since words seemed a bit too weak of a medium to translate how much June appreciated Selena.

The kiss made a smile bloom on Selena's face.

It was nearly ten p.m. when Selena came out of June's room with her dress on, clean but in need of an iron. June felt a pang in her chest. Sure, she appreciated her free time like any other introvert but letting Selena go felt like letting go of the good feeling. She didn't like it.

They hugged again, this time longer and the fit of being between Selena's arms, breathing her almond and vanilla scent, made June want to press a kiss to the juncture between Selena's jaw and neck. She wanted many things, but she eased back, and the soft upturn of her girlfriend's mouth calmed the want to something closer to a wish she'd be fine if it didn't get to happen.

THAT NIGHT, JUNE HAD BEEN IN BED, FRESHLY smelling of her shower gel with Lemon on her left and reading from her e-reader in the dark when her phone pinged.

SelenaSClarke tagged you in a photo.

JUNE SWIPED OPEN TO A PICTURE SELENA TOOK OF Mint and Lemon, perched on the couch and looking at her with a gleam in their eyes. The caption read: "New flavors." The caption was brief and sweet and didn't spark any new fires of worry in June. There weren't many comments yet.

BANAJOON Favorite beings. [sparkle emoji]

DATING SELENA CLARKE COULD ONLY BE DESCRIBED AS comfortable. For the entirety of February and most of March, they saw each other around once a week. Around a week after they held hands, June got even more prom makeup appointments, so she couldn't find the strength to get dressed in more than pajama pants and a sports bra. Hence why Selena would show up twenty minutes after she read June's text with take out.

That sprang a routine of them either eating out in small cafes and fast food joints or going back to Selena's or June's until they finished Avatar: The Last Airbender and began watching one of June's favorite shows - Voltron: Legendary Defender.

As they agreed upon, their relationship online continued its subtle progression. June showed up in Selena's feed whenever they had shoots together. Selena always verified that June was A-OK with any picture she posted. June, likewise, was inspired by Selena's floral dresses and would mention her in various looks where she'd draw entire flowers on her cheeks, collarbones, and even shoulders.

One specific look had June covered in the same pattern of dots, the same pattern of Selena's dress. The posts drew some attention but funny enough, the followers called them "Gal pals" which was endlessly ironic to them.

CHAPTER SIX

BANAJOON

Good job on the shoot! I just saw the behind the scenes in Nadia's Instagram. You looked so good!

SelenaSClarke

thanks! i love her brand so fuckin' much! she just gets what i wanna wear, which is florals and flowy all the time! ! !

BANAJOON

You look amazing in florals. And flowy. And everything under the sun.

SelenaSClarke

yeah yeah keep laying it thick like that [wink-face emoji]

BANAJOON

I'm sorry, I'm just flirting with my girlfriend. [angel emoji]

SelenaSClarke

OMG ! GIRLFRIEND HERE AND YEP SHE LIKES IT
V E R Y MUCH

BANAJOON

And would my girlfriend like to like it even better if my
awkward was accompanied by snacks and cats and a TV
show?

SelenaSClarke

ahhhhhhh that'd have been ideal
but your girlfriend
jfc that made me wanna shriek! yikes! i'm so wow! Okay
lemme finish that thought
i actually got some plans today

BANAJOON

Oh? That's cool!
Can I ask what you're doing?

SelenaSClarke

absolutely! i'm going to see Joey's baby!! !

BANAJOON

Oh, yeah! I saw her post on Instagram!

SelenaSClarke

you follow joey?

BANAJOON

Of course. She's your friend.

SelenaSClarke

aw w w babe! ! you're so soft

BANAJOON

[blush emoji]

SelenaSClarke

yeah i'm gonna go see baby Rin today...

actually...

do you wanna come with me?

BANAJOON

Okay!

Wait.

Are you sure?

SelenaSClarke

ofc!!! fair warning that joey will be extra... smug about how
we got together since she's...

BANAJOON

She's what?

SelenaSClarke

she's known about my gigantic crush on you since like,
december!

BANAJOON

Awh, babe, you had a crush on me?

SelenaSClarke

shhhhh you and that reference of yours have no space

u had a bigger crush on ME!

BANAJOON
You're so right. LOL

SelenaSClarke
anyway! i'm leaving in about, two hours
is that enough time for you?

BANAJOON
You're picking me up?

SelenaSClarke
yep! i always wanted to drive w/ one hand on the wheel and
the other on my precious girlfriend

BANAJOON
Gosh, you're so cute.

SelenaSClarke
too cute?

BANAJOON
Almost.

A sense of déjà vu nearly overwhelmed June when she stepped out of her apartment building and saw Selena in her car. She must have not noticed the interior, when Selena had picked her up for their first date. The sleek black of the paint or the hot red of the interior, but she noticed now. She let a finger skim over the dashboard. Selena watched with something akin to pride in her eyes.

"This is a very beautiful car," June murmured as she leaned in to give her a hug. It had to be short and quick because they were in a car and they were big girls, but June made sure to take in the comforting and now-familiar scent of almonds and vanilla.

"Thank you. I bought it after signing that first contract I got," she whispered since June was still clinging onto her hug. June pulled back with an embarrassed flush, but Selena's soft eyes didn't allow any of it to linger in her system. There was absolutely no space for embarrassment with Selena. She was so sincere and genuine that June's anxiety couldn't even start its shit around her.

"That must have been a pretty big moment."

"It was. I agonized over it for months but then again, I couldn't exist on depending on rides and car services. That was getting so expensive."

June smiled.

"Wouldn't know. I lived here most of my life, so I grew up in these busy streets."

Selena grinned. "Yeah, yeah, show off your street knowledge to this naïve gal who grew up walking everywhere 'cause her hometown was the size of a thimble."

June turned in her seat and watched Selena drive with ease. She had a button-up shirt that she left open over a black dress. It was body-con and made her curves look even sexier. She recalled the kiss she laid on Selena's cheek sometime before she left. She thought of kissing her mouth. Her current lips were glossy and cherry red. June swallowed back her thoughts.

"Was it scary moving to LA?"

"Nah," she replied. "It was the one thing I wanted ever

since I was fifteen. To get out of my small town. To be immersed in more. It sounds pretty cliché, but small towns are suffocating."

There was a hint of something more behind Selena's words. June wanted to know everything. Good or bad. But she hummed and allowed Selena the time to process whether she wanted to say it or not.

"I came out in high school. Not many people even knew what demisexual was. But I did. I am demisexual. But everyone who heard it made some joke that I didn't appreciate so I kept it to myself most of the time. I only told my family and the person I was dating at the time. Fortunately for me, I have an awesome family who never once made me feel wrong for who I am. I tried my best not to end up in a relationship with anyone who would invalidate something that mattered to me."

June bathed in the light that radiated off Selena. She sounded so relieved and happy to share. Also, June felt the very same joy slink its way into her chest and warm her up. Hearing that Selena had good experiences dating and coming out was such a relief.

"I am blessed to have had a good upbringing and a decent childhood but the urge for more stayed. It's why I worked my ass off for my scholarships. It also helped that my mom and older sisters helped me with my education. Whatever loans I had to take were easy to cover once I began to model in college. Apparently, a lot of people liked the look of a fat black girl for their brands."

She said the last with pride in her voice. Even though her words expressed levity, June knew how difficult it must had been for Selena to break through the rigid rules of beauty's standards and to stand out as her authentic self.

"Girls everywhere who are like you must be super proud to have you as a role model," June said.

Selena turned to glance at her while they waited at a red light. "Thank you. It means a lot to affirm that. I have had so many girls in my DMs telling me my activism in the beauty and modeling world has helped them be more vocal about their own goals."

As she spoke, Selena put her right hand, the one she wasn't using to steer, on the gear and remembering her text, June reached to grab it.

Unlike her first attempt at holding Selena's hand, AKA the disastrous juice spill, Selena didn't flinch. She let June play with her fingers, mess with the rings she had on, and finally kiss the back her palm. She threw June a quick glance and June was pleased to see a sheen of something more there. She wrapped both hands around Selena's hand. It felt like she held the most precious thing.

And in a way, it was.

JOEY AND NOOR WERE DELIRIOUS IN A WAY ONLY A PAIR of new parents could be. The baby was swaddled and practically snoring when June and Selena peeked into the crib.

"She's peaceful, surprisingly, since that last week was anything but," Joey murmured. She had been standing behind them by the door, with Noor's affectionate hands around her shoulder. The two looked even closer than when June met them. Joy mixed in the tiredness and it looked so good on them that June sent a tiny prayer to keep their joy close to them for as long as God willed it.

"Enough about my baby, I wanna hear about you two!" Joey practically dragged the two into the living room.

Selena gave June a look that said, "Told you." June shrugged.

"Ahh, I see you got your own eye language there," Noor teased. Selena groaned as she sat down into one of the plush soft chairs in the living room. The place was big, and June admired the simple yet comfortable furniture.

"Not you too. I expected this from your wife but to think you'd betray me this way. Not cool, Noor."

"You know I'm on Jay's side always and forever," Noor murmured and pulled Joey off her perch on the seat to a quick kiss. Joey's cheeks were rosy when she pulled away and she murmured a quick sorry to June.

"Oh, don't mind me. I'm only uncomfortable with PDA when it's me involved," she said as a way of explaining.

But even as she said it, she had been fidgeting with not only her hands, but Selena's as well. Noor and Joey exchanged their own knowing look.

"Stop it you two or no babysitting from Auntie Selena anytime soon," Selena threatened.

Joey's face fell. "I'm sorry! I just am happy to know I was right and you two were a guaranteed thing!" she almost sounded smug. Which made June grin.

Selena groaned. "You promised you'd keep the level of I told you so to a minimum."

"Yeah, but come on, Selena. You two are so cute."

"I agree. Have you been dating since the baby shower?" Noor asked.

Before she said a thing, Selena looked at June. She tried to read Selena's expression, which was a mix of a raised eyebrow and pouty lips, but she was so distracted by how happy she felt to have her relationship validated that she just stared. She was truly useless.

When Selena's mouth, which starred in June's current

daydream, parted in a grin, June shook herself out of the tiny daze.

"Ah..." she failed to remember Noor's question. She gave Selena a helpless look.

"Babe..." Selena murmured with a laugh. She squeezed June's hand and turned to Noor. "Not exactly."

That was answer enough for Noor who just smiled and gave her wife another look.

CHAPTER SEVEN

The first week of April, June had been chilling with Shelby after a long day of work. She might have told Shelby all about Selena and their low-key dates of watching Avatar and Voltron, chilling in their sweatpants, and eating an obscene amount of fast food.

The redhead leaned back and gave June a look then snagged a new pizza slice.

"I'm so jealous of your cute comfy relationship," Shelby grumbled and took a huge bite of their pepperoni pizza. June grinned and munched on her garlic twist.

"It's so sweet it's rotting my teeth," she said once she took a chug of her sprite.

"And rom-com worthy. I'd watch it. But not like in a creepy way."

They had come over, whining about work, which was Shelby's usual mode. June never cared for the reason to why her best friend would show up with a large pizza, she just grabbed them cool cans of Sprite and pressed play on any episode of Parks and Recreation.

"Don't stress, I'm sure you'd skip all the R rated moments."

"Are there any?" Shelby asked after a minute. June, like the ass she was, pretended not to know what they were talking about.

"Any what?"

June didn't mind talking about these things with Shelby. She just felt so protective of how good it felt not to have any worries about sex. It always seemed to her that people, mostly allosexual people, had so many expectations about relationships. When Shelby asked, though, June was sure they were just checking up on June's relationship in their own way.

"R rated moments." They wiggled their brows. June chucked a throw pillow at their head. Shelby evaded the attack but wouldn't let June evade the question. "Well?"

"We held hands and hugged. That raunchy enough for you?" June said.

Shelby sighed. "Sounds heavenly tbh." They said it aloud. Tee-Bee-Eitch. It was weird and endearing as heck. "Where is my dream significant partner when I need them?" They laid back and threw a wrist on their eyes.

"They're waiting for you to publish that newest chapter of your klance fan fic."

"Ha! They probably gave up on it after two chapters," Shelby said with a scoff.

"How dare you insult my future sibling-in-law. They wish they could give you more kudos," June chastised with pizza crust in hand.

"Yeah, yeah, they're probably drawing fanart of chapter fourteen where Lance gives Keith surfing lessons."

"Oh, my god, the underwater first kiss. I can't believe my best friend is the cheesiest fanfic writer ever."

"Shush, you know I'm corny and I love the fluff," Shelby threw back the cushion. June let it hit her in the chest.

"True." She toasted her and took a gulp. Just as she put the empty can on the couch, she got a ping of a notification. Selena's special ping.

"Your soft ace girl?"

"Yep!"

"Gah! I am green with enby," they muttered.

"Get out of here, you punny asshole."

"Whatever. I'm gonna go cuddle your cats who would understand my loneliness now that their mom has a new source of joy."

June stuck her tongue out at Shelby, but they didn't react. They just chased after Mint and Lemon, bribing them with bits of pepperoni (which they proceeded to eat quickly once either cat got close enough).

SelenaSClarke

the launch for spirited cosmetics is in two weeks or so. do you want to come as my plus one?

technically there arent +1s but, the point stands

wanna be my date so u can see huge pics of me wearing the makeup u applied on me and then have junk food?

June gave her calendar a quick look. That'd be a little bit after the middle of April, which incidentally had a comfortable schedule of work that didn't go beyond 5 p.m..

BANAJOON
How romantic!

SelenaSClarke

i am the epitome of romance

BANAJOON
The Fiona to my Shrek
Always making my heart go doki-doki

SelenaSClarke
omgggg nerd!!!!
super nerd....cutest nerd

BANAJOON
Your cutest nerd who's also going to be your +1.

SelenaSClarke
IS THAT A YES?

BANAJOON
YES!!!!

SelenaSClarke
wow exclamation marks. you must be at least raising an
eyebrow now.

JUNE SENT HER A PICTURE OF BOTH HER EYEBROWS
raised and her mouth curled into a grin.

SelenaSClarke
oh my god, an angel, oh wow, 10/10 would date forever

June's heart, the total traitor, banged at the forever but
her traitorous brain also told her it was just an expression.
She was exchanging texts with Selena, more selfies and

mindless back and forth about the most recent season they'd finished of Voltron, when June's attention was snatched by Shelby.

"Can I borrow Mint for a week?" Shelby asked. They had an armful of Mint, who didn't like being held unless he was being petted heavily. Shelby seemed good on their promise to provide said petting. He purred so loud June could hear him from the threshold of the kitchen.

"Yeah, sure. Just make sure your black on black outfits aren't on the floor when he's in a napping mood. He kind of started shedding." As if hearing his mom's slight complaint in her voice, Mint raised his head and gave June a look.

"I don't care. I'd let him shed and shit all over my life. It's already garbage," they grumbled. The second they sat back on the couch; Mint twisted out of their hold. With a sigh, they let him go.

"What's up? Is the block that bad?" June always went with the safest option because she learnt that her best friend was so secretive of their mood swings. She never pushed Shelby to talk just like Shelby never pushed her back.

"Nah. Somehow, writing fanfics is the only thing keeping me distracted," they murmured as they played with their hair. It looked a state as they had been growing it out and it looked ready for a trim.

"Then? What's up?" she nudged Shelby's knee.

"Seasonal depression." They shrugged, not meeting June's eyes.

"You mean yearlong depression?" June tried to joke. The lack of Shelby's usual scoff was alarming.

"Potato, potato." They waved the comment away but that served as June's sign. Shelby seemed like they wanted to talk about whatever's on their mind, but they might need her to be the friend who reminded them.

"Shelbz," at the use of their nickname, Shelby smiled wanly, "You can tell me what's up. You shouldn't let it in, and I won't judge. Have you been seeing your therapist lately?" Shelby looked up from the split ends they'd been inspecting. They gave June a weak nod.

"I've got an appointment in like two days but the very thought of seeing her in this shitty mood is discouraging. I feel like I'm wasting my time. And her time."

"You know that's not true."

After a minute, Shelby shrugged and sighed.

"Yeah. I do." They took a deeper breath and continued, "Therapy is good for me. It allows me to let out all my everyday frustrations. Frustration with my stupid job. Frustration with not taking my chances with my love life."

Halfway there, a couple of tears slipped out of Shelby. Their face turned a peachy shade, accentuating their fiery hair. They took the tissues June passed with a nod of thanks. Wiping away their face, Shelby looked up and just sighed.

"I'm just at an impasse. Something will change soon. It has to."

Shelby sounded so definitive that June didn't know what else she could say. It was good for them to sit in silence but since Shelby kind of professed about something they hadn't felt so great about, June didn't feel good sitting in it.

She got out of her seat and hurried to her modest fridge. She had stocked it recently, thanks to the flux of cash she received from her freelance makeup gigs the past couple of months. Thank god for prom season.

She pulled out some fruits and began making Shelby a milkshake.

When June handed them the cool glass with the colored straw and the extra whip cream, she could had sworn she saw even more tears gather in Shelby's eyes.

"I have some of Selena's cookies too if you like," June offered.

"You're an angel," Shelby replied with a sniffle. June grinned and sat down. She watched them take long drags until their color turned back to normal.

She also recalled a conversation she had with her mother that weekend.

"Speaking of angels, my mom's retiring."

"What?!" Shelby leaned forward.

"Yeah, she told me on the phone two days ago. She says she wants to focus on other things. God help us." She rolled her eyes and Shelby giggled. They both were familiar with June's mom's many ideas.

"So, you know, the bookstore will be hiring a new manager and I know someone," June added pointedly, "who has some experience from college. Also, it doesn't hurt that you have over three years working a marketing job."

Shelby's tear stained face turned a bright happy shade of pink. "Holy shit, are you serious? This could be so momentous. I could be free of my baby supplies hell and, of course, of Karen."

"Fuck Karen," June joined in to say automatically.

"So, yeah, you could and should, maybe, if you want, apply for it." June shrugged. She knew all about being pressured into work opportunities. She felt the pressure the second she finished her second year at college and her scholarship pressure made her pull fourteen hours of studying besides her classes. Hence, why she managed her every job opportunity with nearly freakish attention to how it'd help her future.

"I just might. God, I'm so sick of Karen." Shelby got distracted by Lemon, who sometimes got affectionate when he felt the need for it. Shelby looked like they needed it. Bad.

"And all the books," June pointed out.

"That sounds like a good deal too." A tiny smile bloomed on Shelby's face. It wasn't much but it was promising. Shelby was known for judging June's dangerous attachment to her cats, but they were as weak as June, if not more, to the fur babies.

Although occupied with Lemon's soft purring, Shelby looked up, found June staring at them and winked. They leaned over and the best friends high-fived.

CHAPTER EIGHT

As part of their plan for the launch party, Selena and June met up at a boutique that was one of Selena's affiliations for a while. June found herself slightly sweaty and extremely bothered after not three but five dresses. She always hated trying out clothes in stores. But at least this time her problem wasn't the lack of sizes.

The fitting room was concealed with a thick, albeit easy to move, curtain and the shop had very bright lights that didn't help June ignore the gathering of stretch marks on her belly and thighs. She stopped the fifteenth sigh from coming out her mouth because it wasn't Selena who made her change. It was herself. She didn't see herself in any of the dresses she tried on.

They were pretty. So damn beautiful that her eyes and mouth widened in astonishment that they even came in her size. But still. They didn't stand out as *her* kind of dresses.

"Oh my god!" she heard Selena exclaim. She poked her head out. She'd been barely clothed in boxers and an old bra.

"What's up? You found something?"

Selena had been diligent about finding June her dress, or outfit. June had even tried a suit but did not feel comfortable at all. Plus, she had seen Selena's appreciative eyes on their first date. She wanted to show off her legs.

"Yep! I think you might like this."

The dress she put in her hands was a small black satiny thing with spaghetti straps. It had tiny detail work that shined as June moved it. Before she could attempt to wear it, she chucked off her bra because it wouldn't do. It went on quite easily, which was always a plus with her body getting in the way most of the time.

The bodice had a nice stretch that gave her boobs, as small as they were, a little help looking something not pancake-like. Then in the middle, quite perfectly, it fell open and gave her a little puff of a look. June could hear people's comments about how a girl as big as her shouldn't wear something puffy. But quite honestly? She didn't give a fuck. The low cut in the back also allowed her to show enough amount of skin.

When she felt good enough that all of it settled nicely on her, she opened the curtain. She stood in her battered sneakers and beamed.

Selena was right there, looking as cheerful as she did when she first met up with June. June gave an appreciative gasp and clapped. "That looks absolutely gorgeous." June did not miss the way her eyes clung to every detail. From the abundance of skin showing at her shoulders to her legs. She gave it a little twirl and Selena put a hand to her heart. "You're going to end me. You look so good."

"Thank you." June felt good too.

Deciding on that very one, Selena had no problem procuring it despite June's argument that she could afford it.

Quite honestly, she didn't see herself wearing it again and buying it would have been quite an expense she wasn't prepared for. So, she appreciated that Selena put her foot down and got her the dress for the night.

Since the day was still beautiful out with the April weather providing them with sun and coolness, Selena turned to June with a grin and coyly asked, "Wanna grab a bite?"

June was momentarily dazed by the way the sun reflected all the gold in Selena's eyes, but she managed to nod.

They sat down at a well-known café with a pretty lovely patio-style seating that allowed them to take advantage of the weather. June's mind began to calculate her budget. She had been spending quite a bit more than usual but thanks to her hermit lifestyle, she could afford to go on dates once or twice a month.

The sun had drawn out more patrons. There was a sizable amount of people sitting in tables around them and June noticed some of them turn to look at Selena. She honestly understood their open gazing.

Selena was in a floral romper. Her legs were glistening thanks to her habit of moisturizing often. Somewhere in her mind, June wondered just how she landed Selena's attention. She was just a crusty girl who didn't remember to use deodorant sometimes.

Most of those negative thoughts were expelled when Selena turned her smile to June. She had this incredible gift, which June bet was magic, of turning every topic in June's mind to Selena Selena Selena. If she didn't know it was just her mind doing its usual fixation thing, she would have been disturbed.

"You okay?" Selena asked. She reached across the small

wooden table they snagged by the rail. June turned her palm, so they could slide their fingers together. She smiled down. She was such a sap.

"Yeah. Just wondering how I lucked out this good," she murmured. For once, June was spilling all that was on her mind. And it worked miracles. Selena's cheeks nearly burst from the power of her grin. Good. She deserved to smile that big all the time.

"Funny, I was thinking the same thing," her lovely girl replied. June wanted to scoff. She was nowhere near Selena's magnificence, but knew any self-hatred would only sour the mood. Instead, she just held on tighter to Selena's ringed fingers.

"What can I get you?" The waiter asked. Their eyes practically glued to June and Selena's hands. June, forever anxious, pulled hers away. She forgot for a second that unlike her, Selena was recognizable. It was apparent from the curious looks she generated.

She even noticed someone point a phone in their way in an obvious way. Prickles of discomfort danced on June's body. Her foot began to tap, and her heart sounded suddenly way too loud in her chest. *Holy shit. Please don't let me have a panic attack.* She tried to bargain with her anxiety. If she could have just this one hangout, then she wouldn't do it again. She would be more careful.

Too late. People will find out and you'll get harassed. Selena will get harassed too.

The thought was so unbearable that June's eyes got blurry with anxious tears. What the actual fuck, she wanted to scream. How did her day go so bad so quickly?

"Babe are you okay?" She heard Selena ask. The term of endearment only made anxiety tighten its hold on her.

June opened her eyes and saw the waiter and Selena eying her.

"Yeah. Sorry. Just need the bathroom."

"It's inside," the waiter said helpfully. June didn't recall thanking them, but she couldn't recall much beside the *thump thump thump* in her ears.

Her sneakers sounded so cheap on the floor of the freshly polished café. She wanted to disappear so badly. It didn't help that the inside was crowded, and she had to squeeze between people to get to the bathroom.

One of her bad triggers was her physical entity. The space she took. She wished she could float above the crowd. Alas, someone bumped into her and in her heightened state, June felt the tears fall. *Oh no, oh no, oh no.*

She found herself in one of the bathroom stalls, with her fists tight and pressing into her thigh. She took deep breaths and with every passing exhalation, the tight feeling in her chest, June could feel the panic subside.

Maybe it was the physical distance she put between her and others. Maybe it was the dim lighting in the bathroom lessening the sensory overload. Maybe—

Her thought process paused when she heard the door open.

"June, sweetie?"

Selena. Shit. She totally freaked out.

It's okay. She knew.

"Hey," she replied weakly.

"I'm here. You don't have to come out. Just wanted you to know I'm here."

Selena sounded so calm and not at all like the mess inside June's head. She nodded. Then she realized Selena couldn't see her.

The words nearly choked her, but she got them out,

"Thank you. I'm sorry." She sounded so mousy. *God damn it.*

"It's okay, love. Take your time," Selena murmured. She sounded as if she was in the same room but not close enough.

That felt good. That she didn't crowd her or demand she come out of the stall.

June went back to her coping mechanism. It involved a lot of slow breathing and unfortunately, crying. She knew she'd be a mess but for her, panic attacks were more about feeling like there was a storm in her mind and sometimes the best way was to let it out. She cried, silently, until hiccups shook her body. She didn't mind them except they were kind of painful.

"Here you go," Selena whispered. She put a bottle of water through the opening at the bottom of the stall. June took it with a whispered thanks and gulped some of it down. The perfect temperature cooled her and calmed the hiccups down.

Another fifteen minutes passed, and the worst of the panic moved on. With shaky hands, she wiped her face and unlocked the stall. There was no one outside. She looked around, but Selena was gone.

Her phone pinged.

SelenaSClarke
i'm outside i just wanted to give u some privacy
<3

June typed back a thank you and managed to wash her face and the streaks of tears off. She felt much more balanced when she left the bathroom. And there was Selena. She leaned across the door. Thankfully, the café's patrons didn't seem totally bothered by the way the two hogged the hallways. They didn't even glance at them as they passed June to the bathroom.

Selena's eyes had the usual softness. They didn't ask anything of her, and nor did they show any sign of weariness. A sigh of relief left June's chest.

She didn't want to acknowledge it, but she was terrified she might have scared Selena off.

"Are you ready to go?" Selena asked.

June nodded.

She gestured for them to get out and June followed her. She was confident and drew the attention away from June's hunched walk. June kept her eyes glued to the backs of Selena's thighs. There. That seemed like a good place to focus on until they got to their parked car.

Selena had driven, and it saved June the awkwardness of waiting for a ride. Her mom had needed the car a couple of days ago.

Before June could open her door, she saw that Selena did it for her. She thanked her as she slipped in.

When Selena got into the driver's seat, she didn't move to start the car. It was cool and dry but not suffocating. *Uh oh,* her awful brain thought. *Leave me alone,* June begged.

"Junie?" Selena's nickname for her was like prayer to hear ear. Familiar and comforting.

"Yeah?"

"Are we okay?"

June processed the question. What? She looked up from her lap and turned to see Selena staring at her.

"What do you mean?" she practically whispered.

"Did I... do anything?" Selena sounded so painfully scared that June's arms shot out to grab her hands.

"No. No way. It wasn't you." At hearing the words,

Selena's chest rose and fell noticeably. Her eyes filled with tears, but she was smiling. June didn't know how to translate the reaction.

"Okay. That's good. I'm sorry, I'm kind of freaking out too. I just... I don't want anything to happen to you. I'm sorry."

Now it was June's turn to assure her. "You don't need to be sorry. It wasn't you. It was the crowd. The... stares."

"The stares?"

"Yeah. I saw people staring at us, and the waiter too, didn't help at all. I saw someone point a phone at us. I panicked about us being... photographed." It sounded so bad in her ears. What was she saying? She sounded... ashamed or something.

Hurriedly, she added, "I'm not ashamed of us. Not at all. I just—"

"Junie, babe, it's okay. I understand your worry. I don't approve of being photographed without my knowledge and I'm very open about my life on social media. I can't imagine the level of worry you must have felt. If anything, *I'm* sorry for taking you there."

June practically leapt forward—as much as one could lean in an enclosed space—and trailed her hands over Selena's arms to her shoulders and up her neck. Her face was warm, and her eyes were still glistening.

"Don't be sorry. It's not your fault. It was anxiety's fault. It'll always be anxiety."

"I'm such an ass for making you reassure me," Selena whispered. June shook her head. She hated that Selena felt anything close to negative about herself. She was sunshine and rainbows. But June wasn't delusional. She knew it must have terrified Selena and just because she didn't feel anxiety like June did didn't mean that she didn't worry.

Although June made it practically her job to hide her mental illness from people, for fear of them thinking her a burden, she didn't feel that way around Selena at all.

She trusted her with her darkest moments.

She was honored Selena was this vulnerable around her.

She leaned close and pecked Selena's cheek. Selena's eyes closed, and she kissed June's cheek back.

"I'm sorry I'm crying."

"I was crying just 3 mins ago, I understand."

"I don't want you to feel hopeless with me," Selena murmured.

June leaned back and smiled wanly. She wiped her cheeks with her thumbs. "I know but I can't help it, and neither can you."

"I know. I knew the second I said it that it was unfair of me to ask that of you. Please know I'll try and understand." Selena mirrored June's body language by holding onto June's face.

It centered her.

She nodded.

"Okay."

They stared at one another for a prolonged moment.

"I trust you," June said into the quiet.

Selena nodded. "Thank you."

:☀:

CHAPTER NINE

After she dropped her off the other day, the two maintained their frequent texting. And they even had a long FaceTime chat where Selena directed most of her words to Mint, who had been napping in June's lap.

There was this transformation to their relationship. June felt bare and open and understood. When she remembered the panic attack, she didn't dwell on it, she thought of how Selena held her face and assured her. How she calmed her down by just being there.

It was unspoken that their appearance tonight would be as *friends*. It didn't feel like a lie because to them, their friendship covered a big space of their relationship. They weren't *more than friends*. They were friends with romantic feelings. June knew that's what she felt for Selena. And it was good.

So, it didn't matter to them that people would call them good friends because it was *true*. Plus, how they felt about one another was their own thing. It was one thing for Joey,

Noor, and Shelby to know and a whole other thing for Selena's thousands of followers to be in on their business.

When she slipped into the ride Selena had rented for the night, June felt comfortable. She felt happy. And breathless.

Looking at Selena, sparkly and grinning Selena, was an experience. It was quite visceral. Her heart gave its last performance of a functioning organ and then gave up. Or it felt like it did.

Her dress was lavender and heavenly against her brown skin, looking soft and silky. Her legs looked longer in a pair of sparkly shoes that tapped the floor of the car. She didn't worry about her own pair of comfortable wedges. She was going to have a good time, not a fashionable time. Plus, her dress was stunning enough.

"Junie, you look so lovely," Selena's voice said.

Abashedly, June lowered her eyes. She did wear the dress they painstakingly chose. It was still satisfying to see Selena's reaction all over again, though.

"Thank you."

Her stomach fluttered, and her hand sweat when Selena reached over and fingered the top rings that sat just over June's knuckles. Now that their emotions were at a comfortable balance, Selena was back to being tentative with June. Which she liked. There was something so rich with the way Selena treated her so carefully. As if she was something precious. She liked it.

"Is this okay?" Selena asked quietly. Rather than nod, June turned her palm up and wrapped her fingers around Selena's hand. It was warm as usual. She looked up into Selena's smiling eyes and felt whatever anxious energy left in her system exit through her nose.

"Are you excited?" she asked.

"Oh, kind of?" Selena replied. She laid her head back against the seat gingerly as not to disturb her curls. They looked especially glamorous then. "Although it's not my first campaign, it's still so satisfying to lead something this big, you know?"

"It must feel huge." June rubbed circled into Selena's palm. Her lashes fluttered. June began to understand what that motion meant.

"It does. But it feels less scary with you here with me." Selena's smile was dazzling, and all June could do was stare at her glossy mouth and blush.

Oh, and tighten her grip on Selena. She kind of needed her physical contact in a way she couldn't explain. A thigh scooted to rest against her bare one. Her breath kicked up its speed. Being touched by Selena was a mix of comfort and arousal she anticipated very much.

She felt like she could hold Selena's hand and never worry about her own fingers being too chubby. It felt weird; dating someone who understood her anxieties and insecurities. She had no idea it would be so comforting. Being comfortable with someone wasn't a concept June had known existed for her.

It felt good. So good. To be needed as much as she needed Selena.

It gave her the courage to open her mouth and give Selena the truth. "About the other day," she began. Selena's hand in hers tightened but June smiled to ease her worry. "I regret what happened not because it happened but because it cut our time short."

Selena's hand eased in hers. It was a new language. A language of hands in hands.

"I like being in your presence. You… calm me. Which is not to say I'll never feel uncomfortable and panicky again because nothing could take anxiety away. But it's a good idea to know that when you're around, it's a bit easier to handle stuff."

She sounded so vague she wanted to take back the words. She probably confused Selena and the girl was going to think June was demanding so much of her.

But Selena nodded.

"I like being around you, June. You have this aura of calm—no, believe me—it's so refreshing because I don't have to be totally on. I can be myself." Selena leaned close and June could feel her breath against her face. She hummed in agreement. "I like how slow we are. I don't want us to push ourselves just to meet some hidden schedule. We can be as we wish. No outsiders peeking into our relationship. God knows I'm tired of people meddling in every tiny decision I make."

June frowned at that last bit. She heard the frustration in Selena's voice so clearly. "But that's life. I'm excited that you and I belong to us." Selena's words were so full of kindness that June momentarily lost all capability of responding. She just stared.

Then she grinned.

"That was so perfect. How are you so eloquent all the time? I'm being charmed right off my feet." Selena's face went from thoughtful to amused. She shrugged.

"It felt timely. It felt fated."

"Corny," June teased.

Selena pouted, and June had a sudden thought for her lips.

"Close your eyes, Selena."

She did the opposite and June raised an eyebrow. She

complied then. She looked like the most beautiful thing. Her eyelids glittery and her mouth a rosy pout. June wanted to drink from it.

She leaned closer, inch by inch while she watched Selena's breath hitch. Once she got close enough to feel Selena inhale sharply, June pecked an area just next to Selena's ear. She thanked god she had kiss-proof lipstick on. She leaned back, and Selena eased her eyes open.

"Tease," Selena sounded breathless. Good. Her tone matched June's lack of ability to draw air into her lungs.

Selena snorted and pushed June away a little. Then she pulled her back to her and fluttered her eyes at her. "Do it again?"

"My pleasure, darling." June leaned in again, taking in the faint and addictive scent of Selena's perfume. It congregated behind her ear and June had to use a hand to push the lovely aroma around to get to where the scent was strongest. She dropped a soft kiss there and Selena let out of a soft *oh*.

Somewhere under her heart, and even lower than her stomach, June felt warmth. She felt attraction and it was so good to just lean in again, the sound of her own harsh breathing so loud in her ears, and kiss Selena longer this time. She peppered her neck and ear with those kisses. Selena's hand slipped from hers and it landed on June's bare leg. She squeezed her knee and June breathed out, dangerously close to Selena's collar.

"Kiss me," Selena whispered. "Please," she added, and June's throat dried. She swallowed. She leaned back and found her knees widening their stance, so Selena's hand had more room to run her fingertips. Every touch on her knee, her leg and the area just where her knee met her thigh felt like fire.

June's hand trembled as she slipped it around Selena's waist.

"Is this okay?" she murmured; her eyes half closed but she looked closely for any sign of discomfort from her girlfriend.

Selena nodded. "I've never felt more okay."

With that lightning up her head with sparklers, June confidently ran her hand on Selena's ample waist. She felt the love there and she wondered how many more miracles she would manage to achieve with the girl in front of her. With her free hand, June cupped the area right where her mouth was. It was warm, and she could feel Selena's heartbeat, consistent.

With their mouths coming an inch from touching, Selena's brown eyes fluttered close and her plump lower lip fell to reveal a wetness that June wanted to lick into.

"We've arrived, ma'am," came a voice that jarred both out of the haze of near kissing. June jumped back and so did Selena. They shot a look at one another and holding back a cackle, June smirked.

"Well, I guess we'll just have to pick this up later."

Selena's eyes widened at that and her giving mouth pursed into a thoughtful look.

"Tease."

June laughed and moved to open the door.

SITTING DOWN FOR DINNER LEFT A GROAN COMING OUT of June's mouth. She gave Selena an apologetic smile, but the girl just squeezed her hand and smiled wanly. Two and a half hours of smiling at cameras, socializing, and just having so many voices around her was more than enough for June. Although having the weight of Selena's stare was more than enough to fill her up. She was a tired phone and Selena's presence was a strong power plug. It also helped that everyone was oblivious of how significant the hand-holding was. Everyone was very friendly anyway, so it didn't matter if Selena ran her fingers on June's arm. If she pulled her into a hug whenever she felt overwhelmed. The touches ignited and spread calm through June.

They weren't entirely PG.

June noticed Selena giving her heated looks. The looks were accompanied by a bite of her lower lip and a onceover. June didn't know that being the recipient of Selena's intense focus would feel that way.

Somehow everything came into focus. She was aware of the rise of her chest, of Selena's breath on her ear as she leaned in to whisper something.

Dinner was a regular affair. The food was good, and June strategically laid her thigh adjacent to Selena's, so the pressure would keep her from stuffing her face instead of answering someone's question.

Thankfully, a halal option was available, and she ate without worry. Dessert was the highlight. Chocolate or vanilla, the cake was soft, and drizzled with enough caramel and cream to make her mouth water.

The two shared bites from each other's plates. June was hyperaware of every stare her way but so far no one seemed to think they behaved any differently than any *gal pals*. Besides, having Selena goof around next to her and fret over her lipstick was enough to make her forget that she was being looked at.

Was it any different than the café? Probably not. Did she feel more at ease thanks to how accepting everyone was? Heaps.

There was a knowledge deep in her heart that everyone around appreciated and valued privacy. It also helped that Spirited Cosmetics was owned by a trans woman which made the event exclusive to LGBTQ+ influencers.

Selena was still staring at her lipstick in her compact mirror. June smiled and gestured for her girlfriend.

"Come here, lemme have a look," she said as she nudged Selena's face closer. It felt so casual to just clean up any mess from eating and June saw Selena's eyes widen and her mouth quirk in a teasing grin.

"Can't keep your hands off me, can you?" she whispered. June colored slightly. Bravely enough, she winked.

They were probably too chummy but then again, June's anxiety calmed. Maybe it was the fact she was well-rested. Besides, they were so cute that June wanted to kiss Selena right there in front of the meddling and gossipy circle.

But like the epitome of control, she held back from doing something she'd regret. She watched Selena take loads of pictures and pose with products that had her very same face (except with like flowers and vines) on the campaign photos. It was amazing.

June's limbs felt heavier than usual and once she slipped back into the comfort of the Lyft car, she sank into the seat. Soft music played and as Selena slipped next to her, after what felt like hours of her posing with followers who made it to the event's venue a bit later than advised, June moved to lay her head on Selena's shoulder.

Immediate relief washed over her. Their hands found each other. June let the music strip away the tiredness and closed her eyes. The urge to snatch the heavy falsies off her lids was so tempting but she breathed out slowly and listened to the music and to Selena's breaths.

At a lull in the playlist, Selena tapped June's knee. She looked up.

"Want to come back to my place? Or?"

"Either would be fine. Shelby's babysitting," she said hesitantly.

After a pause in which June bit her lip, Selena smiled. "Your place, right?"

June breathed out an exaggerated sigh of relief. "It's just that I need to recharge, and I miss my kids."

"That's okay, sweetheart, I get it." She leaned over and instructed their driver about the change of plans.

"Plus, I'll make you remove my makeup," Selena said once she nestled back into their cuddle of arms and legs and a lot of comfy fabric.

"That'd be nice."

Selena leaned and placed a kiss on June's forehead.

Sometime between getting out of the venue and into the car, the warm anticipation in June lowered to a comfortable simmer. They leaned against one another, their hands intertwined, and legs crossed at the ankles.

The thought of the almost-kiss and the soft kisses she enjoyed leaving on Selena's soft skin brought back the heat to her cheeks. Selena's reactions to the touches heightened June's pleasure. Her widening eyes and faster inhalation, they were worth it to keep herself on a figurative edge until Selena would ask her so sweetly to kiss her. The whisper, its memory, made chills run down her spine. Mistaking her shiver for a chill, Selena wrapped her arm around June, bringing her closer to her chest. June snuggled closer, enjoying the affection.

It lasted until they found themselves holding hands outside June's apartment. She sighed dramatically at having to let go of Selena's hand to get her keys out.

"Oh, here, I'll help."

June grinned and held up the clutch attached to her wrist, so Selena used her free to get the keys out.

June grinned at her as she pushed her lightly in.

"Hey, y'all early." Shelby said as they came in. They gave June an especially long look, but June let her blush speak.

"We're staying in, Shelbz, thanks so much for cat sitting."

"It was my pleasure. I think Mint spent the whole night in my lap," they said. They demonstrated by pointing at the napping cat.

"Ooph, your legs must be numb as fuck right now."

"I'm practically the Linkin Park song."

Selena laughed at that and sat down so she could have some cuddle time with Mint too. June gave them a smile as she excused herself. Lemon greeted June with a hard look when she stepped into her bedroom.

She shrugged. "I missed you too."

He blinked slowly.

An itch under her skin made June hurry around and remove all the mess that accumulated while she was getting ready. She unzipped her dress, easily too thanks to its material, and got comfortable in a pair of ratty Marvel themed sweatpants and a grey t-shirt.

Letting loose her boobs after a long night of wearing an uncomfortable bra was like heaven. Fuck having perky pushed boobs. Next time she was going to wear her binder.

In the living room, she saw that Mint took over Selena's lap despite her gentle nudges. She must have been worried about her clothes getting coated with his fur. Her fear was rightfully so.

Shelby, however, was quite comfortably munching on

cookies. When June gave them a pointed look, they hurriedly got to their feet.

"Here, let me have him. He doesn't accept that not everyone sports that 'I was sat on by two cats for three hours' look." Shelby scooped the striped furry beast into their arms. He meowed at them, but Shelby gave him a soft peck.

The second they laid him on the floor by the couch he darted into the kitchen, surely ready to break something as revenger.

"Oh well, I deserved it," Shelby muttered after Mint.

June and Selena watched them with fascination.

"Okay then! Since Mint's forgotten how many times I scratched behind his ears and had to see his butthole, I'm gonna head out." They gave a salute to which both Selena and June waved.

"Bye, Shelby, it was nice to meet you!"

June gasped.

"Oh my god, this was your first meeting and—"

"Pfft, June, you realize we're mutuals on Twitter and Instagram, right?"

"I read Shelby's fic basically every week, babe," Selena murmured. June looked at her, seeking assurance that she didn't just totally forget to introduce the girl she is dating to the person who knew her best.

"You're okay," Selena mouthed while Shelby came close and tentatively took June's hand. June nodded. "Hey, bud."

"I'm sorry. It has been a night." She let out a deep breath and with it expelled some of the static that got her all tied up together.

"Cool. Cool, cool, cool." Shelby pulled June into a hug and June, already comfortable with Shelby's tactile self, hugged her back.

"Thanks for cat-sitting, again, friend."

"No worries. Just continue to feed me cookies!" they directed that at Selena and Selena gave her a thumb-up. They left after a quick show-down where they nuzzled Lemon and Mint despite the felines' reluctance. Once the door closed, June looked around.

"Babe," Selena said. The sound pulled all of June's strings. She turned and saw Selena petting the couch next to her.

It wasn't even a conscious decision. Her body just followed instructions. She slid right into Selena's open arms. They wrapped around her head and she let out a giggle right into Selena's cleavage.

"This is the best place I've ever laid my head," June whispered.

Selena laughed and swatted her back gently. June laughed with her. Then she sighed and got even closer. Selena's sigh of contentment was all she needed for her eyes to get incredibly heavy. Thank god for her makeup remover. She didn't have a stitch of product left and hence no worry at all about dozing off.

"Hello, babe, I kind of need to get changed and cleaned up."

June whined softly and at Selena's laugh she grinned up at her. Her brown eyes looked so bright that close. June dropped a kiss to Selena's collar and Selena's lashes fluttered.

"Do you want to stay the night?" she asked attentively as she gave Selena the chance to get up and stretch.

"Depends." She smirked. June tilted her head.

"On what?"

"If you remove my makeup?" Selena said playfully.

"Sweetie, it'd be my honor. Also. I want you to," she

finished with a sober look. She needed Selena to know that she had craved sharing her space with Selena in every aspect allowed so early in their relationship. She wanted to wake up wrapped up in Selena's almond and vanilla scent, and possibly her arms too.

"Are you sure?"

"Yes. Stay." June reached out and Selena took her hand. She led her to her bedroom.

Once inside, June turned and saw that Selena began to slowly unzip her dress. The material gave away and fell to the floor. June's eyes ate up the lacy bra, down Selena's belly, which was soft and rippled with stretchmarks, very much like her own. Selena's thighs were so lovely and thick June wondered what they'd feel like around her shoulders. June swallowed harshly.

Selena stood in June's bedroom in nothing but thin and lacy underthings, her hair done, and her makeup flawless. June swallowed and tried to maintain the flirty tone.

"I'll need pajamas," Selena said quietly.

Lemon was nowhere to be seen. June suspected he joined Mint in the kitchen. She turned to her closet and got a different pair of worn soft sweatpants and printed t-shirt.

"Got 'em," she said as she handed them to Selena. Selena smiled and laid them on the bed.

"A toothbrush?"

June rushed to the adjoined bathroom and found the emergency toothbrush she had in the cupboard.

Selena smiled and turned to get dressed. It almost was too much of a relief. June had never been naked around anyone. She could feel the anxious energy eating her up.

"By the way, I'm like not sex repulsed but I don't really care for it."

Selena's voice pulled June out of her tumulus thoughts.

"Oh." She let the smile of relief invade her face. Her shoulders dropped. "Me too. I mean, I'm pansexual but like, super anxious about sex?"

Selena's tentative smile turned full on.

"That's great. Except... I need skin care products," Selena trailed off.

"Who do you think I am?" June hiked up an eyebrow at that. Selena laughed.

"I was just kidding!" She still took the liquid makeup remover and disappeared to clean up her face. In the meantime, June's Capricorn-self got her hanging Selena's dress up. When she settled into bed, after making sure the cats were comfortably in their beds in the kitchen, June took a deep breath and waited for Selena.

"Was everything okay?" June asked Selena the second she peeked her fresh face out of the door. She was luminous. In the dim light of June's night reading light, she couldn't help but marvel over how intimate it felt to have Selena wear her clothes—again!—and sit in her bed.

"Yeah. You use a good brand. I had to loosely braid my hair that's why it took me a while," she explained as she smoothed the comforter by her thigh. June noticed the change of hairstyle. The curls were braided back, bringing Selena's full cheeks and soulful eyes into focus. June noticed Selena's quick glances at the empty spot next to her.

"Come here. Get your fluffy butt over here. Cuddle me," she said. She also pushed back the comforter. Selena smiled impishly.

"You're so bossy, Junie," Selena replied as she crawled on all fours towards June. June's heartbeat quickened.

"You like it," June murmured once Selena was close enough that her breath, minty fresh, breathed on her cheek.

She nodded at the question in Selena's eyes. Selena leaned down. She pecked June's cheek.

June sighed, and she laid back some more, making Selena gently lower herself on top of her. It allowed June to feel Selena's chest against hers and her warm mouth right where her neck and ear met.

The silence was comfortable and cut through with the soft inhalations June took whenever Selena's lips touched somewhere sensitive. She braced her hands next to June's head and sat atop June's legs. Her weight felt like perfection. June wondered if that was what weighted blankets felt like. She pulled Selena closed by jiggling her knees, which made Selena yelp and laugh.

"Oops, I almost fell on your mouth." Selena winked. She braced herself and looked into June's eyes.

"Unfortunately, the keyword is *almost*." June slid her hand around Selena's hips and felt the strip of skin between her pants and t-shirt. When she tickled it, Selena squirmed but didn't pull away.

"Hm, are you looking into changing that into *definitely*?" Selena leaned down and pressed her full mouth so close to June's own that the tease felt unbearable. She now understood how Selena might had felt in the car when June was the one doing the teasing.

"Yes. Kiss me, Selena," she breathed out.

Their lips touched. Soft on soft. The meeting of lips so warm that it made June's entire face feel as if it was set on fire.

The slow movement of Selena's lips against hers sent shivers into every nook and cranny of June's body.

She brought her hands higher, caressed Selena's sides until the girl atop her murmured her name into her mouth.

That brought the wetness of her tongue closer to June's mouth. She took a breath, opening for Selena.

The first lick into her mouth made June's eyes roll to the back of her head and she tightened her hold on Selena and hummed.

It was so easy to open her mouth and let Selena take charge. Lick and mouth at her lip. It felt like worship. It felt like Selena found June's taste and was trying to memorize it.

June's entire body felt so hot she worried about melting into the mattress. But she kissed back. Licked into Selena's mouth with the same vigor she received. She moaned when Selena bit her lower lip. It was soft and faint but still made June's clit throb.

Selena pulled away then, leaving June breathless and clutching onto Selene's hips as if they were her rope to safety.

"Was that okay?" Selena asked.

"Yes."

"Did you like it?"

"I love it," she breathed. Selena smiled at her, brilliant and lovely, and June felt so thankful she went to that baby shower party and watched the beautiful woman atop her bed prepare cupcakes.

They stared into one another's eyes and Selena leaned down to peck June's mouth. The heat was there but there was no urgency, no hurriedness. Selena's mouth was so delicate on hers June felt like eating it up.

"Me too," Selena whispered back. June closed her eyes in content. They hugged then, overwhelmed and aware of how kissing wasn't just a step towards more. It filled her veins with just the right amount of energy. Kissing was good and perfect just for them.

"Is it okay if we stop here?" Selena asked when she

comfortably laid next to June. She rested her head atop the extra pillow. Her hand rested under her cheek. June mirrored her position.

She nodded. She was exhausted too and the tiredness from the car ride came back. It was a night. Hectic and draining but so much fun. She reached and thumbed Selena's lower lip. Selena grinned at her.

CHAPTER TEN

J une had shared a bed once when she was eighteen with her at-the-time best friend who had to stay over because of transportation issues. She didn't feel comfortable that one time. She buried her face in the pillow and once she got tired of tossing and turning, she got up and just sat in the living room until Daniella's parents could pick her up. When June's mom saw her watching cartoons at five AM instead of in her bed sleeping, she didn't ask. She knew June's intense need for private space wasn't being met.

Waking up in a bed with Selena though was a whole new different experience. First, she didn't wake up until her accountability alarm at 9:30 AM rang. Second, she was smooshed into Selena's chest and she didn't mind it. Not one bit.

"You have a big bed," Selena murmured into June's hair. June smiled.

"I like my space."

"It's convenient too. Do you share it a lot?" At the question, June raised her face to look at Selena. She had a pensive look but kept rubbing on June's back.

"I mean, yeah," she said with a smile. She meant her cats, but Selena gave her a long look. Narrower than usual. June realized with a pleased start that Selena was jealous. "Hah, you're cute when you're fake jealous. Also, no. My last relationship was long distance and I was in college. No way of affording to meet up often."

"You never dated in college?" Selena wound a finger around one of June's curls which escaped her bun.

"I went on dates, but I don't know. No one ever clicked." June traced Selena's nose with a finger then her mouth, Selena smiled and kissed her fingertip.

"What about you? Share your bed with lotsa people?" June asked. The question felt harmless enough and June was curious. Selena didn't seem bothered by it. She shrugged.

"Kind of? I don't know. I feel so much so quickly, so my attraction is all over the place. But not in a while. It has been difficult with the whole public figure thing," she replied.

"Soon to be actress too," June reminded her.

"Ha! That too." Selena adjusted until June was nestled on the pillow and Selena's arm had the chance to regain the feeling. She winced but waved June's apology away.

They laid there, thighs touching, soft on soft making June smile. She wondered how come she never knew that the reason she felt so bad about being close to people was because they weren't like her. She was too self-conscious of her body. But with Selena, whose body was so much like hers, it felt okay. Whenever Selena pressed against her or hold her it felt like comfort times a hundred.

"Are you nervous?" she asked. Selena's nerves showed in the way she chewed her lip.

She smiled at June and whispered, "So nervous." That was June's cue to pull Selena into her arms. Selena fit under her chin perfectly.

"It will be my first ever role that has lines. I'm so ready to be someone else. Someone with a name. Not some background waitress or whatever." Selena sounded both frustrated and scared. June looked down at her. She met the brown eyes with as much confidence as she could muster.

"You're gonna be amazing."

"You think so?" June's never heard Selena sound that unsure. She brushed a kiss on her brow.

"I know so. You were born to inspire." She felt it in her very being, how right it was for Selena to be a role model, to be someone that fat black queer girls everywhere looked up to.

"Thank you, Junie. It means a lot," Selena whispered, and June kissed her forehead again. She began to pepper kisses all along Selena's face and cheeks and mouth that Selena giggled.

"Stop, you're going to get me all emo," Selena whined.

June sniggered. "Sorry, you're just so irresistibly cute in the morning."

Selena fluttered her lashes. "Cute enough for you to make me breakfast?"

"Abso-fucking-lutely." June smacked one last kiss on Selena's cheek. After a moment's consideration, she leaned in again to kiss Selena's other cheek. Her mouth made a smacking noise and she quite liked it, so she repeated the kisses until Selena began to giggle and swatted at her softly.

"Stop, you're gonna make me want to make out and I

have morning breath," she said quietly, though she leaned into June's body and wrapped an arm around June's waist.

June didn't even spare one thought of anxiety to how closely their breaths entwined and how she could feel Selena's thigh against her own and she was the most self-conscious person she knew.

"I don't care. Do you?" she propped herself on her elbows and gave Selena a look. The woman was so lovely with her t-shirt riding up, June wanted to kiss her belly and make Selena get even antsier. Her hair was perfectly secure in its braids. June got distracted by that. "Is it okay to sleep without covering your hair? I hear from black people that it dries their hair out."

Selena groaned. "It's not. But I couldn't expect you to have a silk cap."

"Oh." June shelved that in the back of her head. Then leaned in and kissed Selena on the cheek one last time. "Sorry."

"Don't worry about it. It was just once. Not wearing a cap to sleep meant I wouldn't wake up in the middle of the night freaked that it fell off, so that was a plus in a way," Selena added with a smile.

"Speaking of, it's strange that Mint and Lemon didn't hound us for food. I never make it to 9:30 a.m. without them waking me up at 4 a.m.," June thought aloud. She eased herself back on her side. They laid there facing each other, talking quietly.

"About that," Selena started. She looked guilty. "Lemon woke me up and I fed them."

"You did? What time was it?"

"It was around six?" Selena looked so cute with a thoughtful look on her face.

"Oh, that's perfect." June smiled at her. She felt her face grinning nonstop. God, was that what happy felt like?

"You're not mad at me?" Selena asked quietly.

"Absolutely not." June leaned and kissed Selena's cheek.

Selena huffed again. June giggled and basically dragged herself out of bed. "Okay, time to deliver on that breakfast."

"I'd whine about you leaving me, but I really don't mind," Selena said. June heard the smile in her voice, and she decided Selena's punishment for being uber-cute was going to be her two cats darting into the room and taking over the bed.

Three minutes into whisking eggs for plain scrambled eggs, June heard the footsteps walking close. She smiled immediately when Selena wrapped her arms around June's stomach. She leaned back and received the minty kiss somewhere on her neck. What also came with Selena was two menaces. They meowed endlessly as they smelled the food cooking. June gave them a stern look, but Lemon didn't care. And Mint eyed the counter with an especially calculating look.

"Uh-oh, he's going to ju—" Mint jumped, scaring June.

"No! Mint, no!" she reprimanded and immediately got him off the counter. She locked him with Lemon in the bathroom, which was the only place she could since Lemon had an issue with having his box behind a closed door.

When she went back to the kitchen, Selena had taken care of making tea.

"Hope you don't mind me intruding."

"Not at all," June said as she got back to preparing the eggs. Once the tea was on the kettle, Selena went back to snuggling June's neck.

"Your cats are relentless." Selena murmured into her

hair. She might have been complaining but June heard the affection in her voice.

"You're lucky they didn't follow you into the bathroom," she replied as she let Selena nuzzle her neck some more.

It sent a shiver down her spine and made her limbs relax even more. Momentarily, she forgot about what she was doing. With a huff she pushed Selena back with her butt. Selena playfully swatted at June's butt with a kitchen towel she probably grabbed from the counter. June carefully let the eggs cook enough for them to be perfectly scrambled yet not entirely done to the level of them being dry.

Despite her previous complaint, June found Selena back on the couch, giving her a sense of déjà vu, with Mint and Lemon on her lap.

With two plates in her hand, she sat down. Selena had helped by pouring orange juice into a glass for June and a deep mug of milk tea for herself.

"Once, Mint watched me shower. I was too tired to kick him out and honestly, his every two minutes meowing kept me from falling asleep under the water."

"Wow, Mint to the rescue," Selena said around a forkful. She hummed appreciatively in intervals and it just gave June a big head about her mediocre egg making skills. She also buttered some toast which they scarfed down. She seemed to adore the milk tea.

"What are you up to today?" Selena asked.

June went through her mental calendar, which she had a physical copy of and an electronic one on her phone. Yesterday was one of them.

"Today's my day off and tomorrow I've got some appointments."

Selena hummed in response, distracted by Lemon trying to grab a taste of her breakfast.

"What about you?" June watched Selena's face scrunch as she whispered no to Lemon's incessant nature. She looked up and smiled.

"I have a fitting around two thirty p.m. but I'm free right now."

The clock read around ten twelve a.m.

"Do you want to do something or...?" June finished up and let Selena take both empty plates to the sink. She didn't mind Selena cleaning up. She watched from the couch as her girlfriend donned gloves.

"I actually was going to check the reaction from last night. I hadn't had the chance before bed because," she paused meaningfully and gave June a look. There was absolutely no need to remind June of why they were distracted from their phones the previous night. The heat of Selena's stare was enough to remind June of waking up with the feeling of bruised lips. It was amazing. She licked said lips and Selena's eyes widened comically.

With an eyeroll, June joined her by the sink and helped her dry the plates and cutlery as well as their glasses. It was such a domestic scene June's brain was high on endorphins. That and the morning medication she took.

"I've always been fascinated by the way you interact with your followers. You're like, always gracious. I don't know how you have the temperament."

"Sweetie, that's just a lot of fake smiling as I hit the block button. Also, it helps that sometimes I just log out and let my agent handle stuff."

That gave June something to think about. She took a while to formulate her thoughts.

"So, in the future, if we did ever make *us* public, do you think it'll be a giant mess?"

Selena's head tilted as she considered her question.

"June, I don't think of us as a mess. Us happening has been the most—I don't know, is it insulting if I say comfortable?" June shook her head. "Then yes. Comfortable describes us so well. I have fun with you but also know I can be myself which is just a bear in hibernation." She nudged her hips to June's playfully.

"In the future, when you're comfortable with being in the spotlight of people's nosiness, we won't be a mess."

At the words, a piece of June's mind, which had been preoccupied with her panic attack the other day and how it might affect Selena's opinion of her, calmed down.

They finished up the dishes quietly, June's mind, like always, was still contemplating how Selena's own description matched hers. In a mind that rarely rested and was always hyper aware of the smallest chance of fucking up, June appreciated the space she had with Selena in which they could be relaxed.

It inspired her with this need to kiss her girlfriend.

So, with gloves on, a pillow crease on her face, and tea on her breath, June leaned in and kissed her lovely Selena. Selena smiled immediately against her mouth, closing her eyes, and leaning into the embrace. Since Selena's hands were technically busy, June pulled Selena closer by the hips. Ample and clothed in her soft pajamas, they fit so well against her own. June didn't feel one ounce of self-consciousness at having her chest press against Selena's. The feel of their heaviness might have made the tightening in her stomach get a tad bit more intense, but she was happy with nipping at Selena's mouth, licking Selena's lips, and sucking Selena's tongue into her mouth.

With a huff, they pulled back, June still had Selena in her arms, her thumbs pressed into Selena's back and she heard the huffed moan Selena let out as June continued to massage her back lightly. With every moan June got from Selena's mouth, June pushed her lightly until she had Selena pinned loosely against the counter. The air felt heavy post kisses. June trailed feathery kisses from Selena's ear down to her neck and the lovely smell there was so very Selena that it made June take a taste. Selena practically buckled. Her knees failing her, probably. June supported her by bringing her closer and trying that move again.

"That feels so good, Junie," Selena breathed out.

"You feel so good," June said back.

With a dreamy look in her eyes, glazed and half-mast, Selena took off the gloves, put them down somewhere behind her and with determination, placed her hands around June's jaw. She pulled her closer and took charge. She kissed June so hard, it was June's knees' turn to buckle. Selena chuckled but continued to nip at her lower lip. The give and take of plush lips against her increased the fire in June's stomach from simmer to raging. She groaned as Selena turned them around and pressed her against the counter. That combined with Selena's mouth and hands on her made June moan so loud she pulled back and embarrassedly bit her mouth.

"That was really hot, Junie," Selena murmured. She kissed the hand that June raised to cover her face with.

"Says you," she whispered and nudged Selena's cheek with her nose. Selena grinned and turned her head to kiss said nose.

"I think we just peaked at cutest moment ever, don't you think?"

June giggled. "Yep. Definitely."

With one last kiss, which left June's throat dry and lips buzzing, Selena winked and pulled away. They settled on the couch after that, Selena's legs in June's lap, scrolling through endless comments of endearing fans. While Selena went through dozens of comments about Spirited Cosmetics and Selena's campaign photos, June grabbed a paperback and began to read. At some intervals which Selena had to take due to the size of interactions she received, June would read her some lines from the book.

Some were hot, some were dreamy, and Selena's reactions always made June grin. She had read a hundred pages when Selena determinedly clicked her phone close and put it down.

"I'm done here for the rest of the day," she told June as she leaned over the tiny couch to peck her cheek. "Are you reading a sexy scene? Read it for me?"

June giggled. "No way."

"Come on. Read me some filth."

"It's not even filthy. Just... extremely adorable."

Succumbing to Selena's deep eyes, June let the girl curl in her lap, resting her head under June's chin. She read her a scene in which a heroine lost her shit over the hero's nipple piercing. Just as the plot thickened with angst, June's stomach groaned.

"Hey, do you wanna order in—" The sound of the door unlocking interrupted June. There were two people who had a key to her place besides herself. Shelby and her mom.

"June," came the call of her mother. With a wide-eyed look, Selena sat up from June's lap. June braced herself.

When her mom, Zahra Saeed, in all her rounded figure clad in a deep mauve shoulder-abaya came into the living room, hearing her say: "I've got you some pickles," was the last thing June expected.

:☼:

CHAPTER ELEVEN

It was almost anticlimactic. Zahra gave them one look and held up the tote bag. It looked heavy, so June hurried and took it. Inside she found around four jars of Irani pickles that were only sold two blocks away from her mother's apartment.

She felt Selena's tense body against hers when she sat back down but she also saw the disarming smile on Zahra's face.

"Selena, this is my mother, Zahra Saeed. Mama, this is Selena Clarke. My girlfriend." At that last word, she instinctively reached for Selena's hand. It clutched hers so tightly and she gratefully clutched right back.

"Pleased to meet you, Selena. I'm sorry to bother you on such a lovely day."

Her mother's English always had that infliction of having it learnt as a second language and June smiled at the way she spoke so formally.

"The pleasure's all mine, Ms...uh," Selena trailed off.

"Oh, call me... Khala! That'd be good for now." Zahra quirked an eyebrow and June wanted to roll her eyes.

Almost knowingly, Zahra gave June a grin. "I was just dropping that off but now I'm kind of craving some shawarma. Do you girls care to join me?"

"Mama, it's okay—" June had started.

"I'd love to, Khala!" Selena said at the same time. With a lingering smirk, Zahra gave Selena a wider smile and nodded. June, however, was glued in her space because Selena was being such a kiss-ass to her mom. It warmed her extremely.

"Well then. June knows my favorite place. Should I give you twenty minutes to change?"

"WE DON'T HAVE TO DO THIS TODAY, BABE." June pulled on a pair of comfortably worn pants. The ripped jeans effect was kind of exaggerated, but she covered the biggest of rips with a long button up shirt. She rolled up the sleeves and grabbed a hair brush. She was moving so quickly while Selena carefully applied lipliner.

"Babe, you called me babe. Aw," Selena drew out the sound.

"Sweetie, can you please focus?" June said in a fake exasperated voice.

Selena grinned. "Now, I'm sweetie? Please ease up, my heart cannot handle all this soft." She sat staring up at June with a hand on her chest and a soft smile on her unfinished drawn lipliner until June literally had to lean down and kiss her. Finding reasons to kiss Selena's soft mouth was becoming one of June's favorite things in the past twenty-four hours. They both giggled for a minute.

"I want to. I'm kind of freaked out but she seems very

chill for an Arab mom." Selena was concentrating now on her eye makeup.

"Oh yeah, my mom's bi," June said offhandedly.

She turned from her closet due to the sound of Selena's shocked gasp.

"What? You didn't tell me that!" Selena said a little too loudly and had to hush herself halfway through her sentence. She looked wearily at the door.

"I—uh, I guess it slipped my mind. She's never been not bi to me. Guess I took it for granted to have a queer mom." June sat down to get some socks on.

"And she's known you're pan for how long?"

"Uhhhhhh, I never really came out to my mom? She always knew from my Instagram, I guess. We just never had the talk. We surprisingly talk mostly about food and Turkish TV shows that she ropes me into watching."

Selena gave her a look. Her mouth was in a small O and her eyebrow hiked to her hairline. June called it Selena's "shocked" face.

"You have the coolest mom."

June laughed weakly. "You could say that."

Once Selena loosely tucked the graphic t-shirt that June handed her into the pair of pants also borrowed from June's closet, the two had spent twenty-five minutes going through the motions of "should we panic? Nah."

Zahra was on the couch, her hijab loosened as she browsed June's print library.

"You two are ready! Excellent! Let's go in your car, June. I took an Uber!" Her mom said with so much enthusiasm June wanted to cringe. Until she saw Selena's huge grin. She really seemed to enjoy her mom's ability to talk like a dangerously caffeinated person with the scarily wide eyes and constant smiling. June used to wish she had some of her mom's enthusiasm for life. Then she lost her dad and June found out her mom had been truly happy and had to reconcile so much when she lost the love of her life.

"Mama. Stop using Uber. You can use my Lyft account."

"Doesn't matter to me. Come on, let's head out. Are your cats fed?" Zahra directed the last at June. June nodded. As they left the apartment, her mom began her questioning. They were all genuine questions at least and none of them made June want to jump in and stop the conversation. Behind them, June saw Selena give her excited grins in between steps as they exited the staircase.

The drive consisted of June going back and forth as her mother and Selena continued their conversation. They got along well. June had known about her extended family in the Middle East though they couldn't really afford to visit them often. Selena talked about her sisters and how exciting it was to be supported by her family when she pursued acting. Zahra peppered in questions about her family, finding out about Selena's youngest child position.

"Well, they should! You're a bright young lady. I've seen your pictures in Sephora and I'm quite impressed with your campaign pictures," she said with so much confidence that June grinned from ear to ear.

Selena clutched June's hand that was resting on the gear between them and smiled beautifully at Zahra.

"Thank you."

Her mom was quiet after that, giving June and Selena a moment to look at one another. The place was a small shop, but it was a spot June and her mom frequented so much the staff were familiar to them. Narmeen, a tall cashier, greeted them in Arabic.

"Ahlan, ahlan!" *Welcome, welcome.*

Zahra chit chatted as June and Selena got into a table. The place had two other families, so June wisely got a table far from the one with the little baby.

"I think your mom is hitting on the waitress," Selena whispered and June grinned.

"I think so too," she replied. Their whispers were interrupted with Zahra giving them a fond look. June leaned away and didn't bother fighting the blush on her face. Her mom read her well. Despite having a relationship best described as "okay," Zahra almost freakishly knew June.

"Will you be having your usual?" Narmeen asked and June turned to Selena.

"Our usual is a platter of chicken and beef Shawarma. They have other stuff. Do you wanna peruse or?"

"Shawarma is great. I'll have that!"

At that, Zahra smiled a secret smile. June knew that her mom loved feeding her friends. She'd always leave after her weekly visit with lots of those butter cookies that Shelby liked.

"So, tell me. Are you going to be my daughter-in-law?" the second the words came out of Zahra's mouth; June groaned softly and hid behind her hands.

Selena chuckled. "I think we're a bit early for that, Ms. Zahra."

"Call me Khala, Selena habibti," she reassured, tapping Selena's hand on the table twice. Selena tucked her chin into her chest and smiled. She was so lovely; June couldn't help but stare.

"Mom. Selena and I are dating. It's only been around what—almost three months?" she said the last with a look at Selena. Selena nodded.

"But I've kind of liked you for almost six months," Selena said. At that Zahra quirked her eyebrows.

June just stared. She knew that. But why did the butter-flies in her stomach go into an uproar? She wanted to kiss Selena right there. They got interrupted by their drinks. Zahra engaged Narmeen in small talk as June nudged Selena.

"Hey, if my mom wasn't right there, I'd kiss you."

Selena's lashed fluttered coquettishly at her. Before she could reply, though, Zahra said, "you know I have nothing against PDA, June."

June blushed at that and spluttered but both Selena and Zahra grinned and sipped their drinks.

"Anyway, I'm not going to bother you about that. I know my daughter and I know she's cautious. I just might have seen a lot of you on my feed last night and thought I'd drop by," Zahra said. She had a look on her face as she rested her chin on her propped-up hands. She looked happy for June.

"Shokran, Mama. It means a lot to have your support."

"Akeed. You're my daughter and anything that makes you happy, which is in this case is you, Selena, I'd welcome with open arms," she replied. She reached over with her right hand to grab June's and with her left to grab Selena's.

"I see a lot of joy in your eyes. Both of you. I'd love to get to know you more, Selena, so don't be a stranger and anytime you need someone to make you balaleet, I'm your khala, okay?"

Although Selena couldn't have known what balaleet was, she nodded.

"Yes, Khala." Selena sounded almost near tears. June was emotional too and a tear spilled over when Zahra put their hands atop one another. It felt like a mountain they got over together. It might have been small and totally unex-pected, but it was the push June sort of needed to fit Selena into her life with an unwavering assurance.

"Now, enough talking and eat up. This is on me because I'm a rich Arab." Despite June's argument with her mom that she wanted to chip in, Zahra insisted.

"So, is this like an Arab thing?" Selena whispered to her while Zahra was busy, once again, chatting up Narmeen.

"Not being able to let another person pay for a meal? Yep."

"Nice!" Selena whispered with a grin. With a bit of grease on her lower lip, her eyes crinkled in a smile, that's when June knew. She was falling in love with Selena Clarke.

CHAPTER TWELVE

A sweaty Selena was great. A smiling, slightly heaving Selena was even better. June grinned as she propped herself with her pillows. It was almost eleven PM and her back whined from the six hours of work she just endured. Sure, the wedding party looked kind of stunning and June was riding the endorphins of a job well done, but her body hated her at that moment.

"You look so happy, babe," she murmured. She saw her half-lidded eyes and opened them wider. Selena had sneaked an hour after her rehearsals just to FaceTime.

Filming the paranormal drama TV show meant training. Meant working close to 18 hours a day. Selena was so wiped out that June saw her once more after their trip to the Shawarma place where they spent an hour just chatting about Selena's upcoming busy schedule and kissing in intervals.

Kissing was so much fun. It didn't feel like a stepping stone to something else. It felt like a destination all on its own. There was no hurry. Besides the hurry of getting their mouths on one another.

They'd lain down and there'd been a heat rising between them but as if in an unspoken agreement, they'd pulled away before they got too heated. June appreciated that. Being a virgin didn't matter much to her. It was a well forgotten social construct. But she was anxious. Sex made her anxiety flare up.

Those moments when June tasted Selena on her tongue and would feel the bite from her teeth on her lower lip. Those moments meant so much. June would close her eyes and murmur sweet nothings and watch Selena's eyelashes flutter. It was her sign of blushing. Her skin felt so hot to the touch June couldn't keep her hands off her face. She kissed the dimples and the smile lines, then the smile itself until they were so engrossed in their making out that an actual alarm Selena had set up for her to leave would go off.

Looking at Selena's smiling face, her brows shiny with moisture and her hair tied back to keep it from getting messy thanks to the physical exertion, it made June's heart pound with a familiar four lettered feeling.

"It's weirdly fun to be pushed to a new level. I mean, I do work out, but this isn't regular work out. For a minute there today, I kind of wanted to kick my trainer in the face."

"If he says one fatphobic comment I'm ending him," June nearly growled.

"He's just pushy. But the second we're done with the training he's like all smiles and cozy encouragement. This guy watches too much reality TV. Niceness works, buddy!"

Selena was in her changing room, away from the cast members, and June giggled at the viciousness in her girl-friend. God, she was amazing.

"Well, know that I'm behind you every step of the way if you did want to end him. I've seen Breaking Bad, I'm bad."

Selena laughed, and with eyes turned into crescents and her mouth stretched across her lovely face, she stared at June. For a second there, June's cheeks heated up and she huffed a laugh.

"I'm glad to know my body still reacts as if we'd just met. God, I'm such a fangirl."

"Aw, babe, you can't help that you had a crush on me," Selena crooned.

"We're dating," June deadpanned. A smile broke into her face though.

"Still."

They grinned at each other there until Lemon jumped onto June's chest and got Selena cooing and talking in a high-pitched voice. Her baby voice was basically as if she'd breathed helium. June let her try her best to get Lemon to look at the camera, but he stubbornly and forlornly stared into the distance.

"Someone's moody and probably misses me."

"Are you talking about me or Lemon?"

"Aw, you miss me?" Selena tilted her head and gave June her usual teasing look. Mouth in a kissy face and her eyebrows moving up and down. On anyone else, it might have looked ridiculous, but June just smiled and took a screenshot.

"I thought that was obvious by my Instagram story."

June had shared some selfies that she had saved from their cozy movie night in dates and their Spirited Cosmetics launch. The followers count went up so much for June in the past week that she was half-terrified and half-impressed.

"Junie, watching your story was like the equivalent of listening to a mixtape made just for me. It was lovely. Like you, girlfriend," Selena assured.

"It's what you deserve," June responded. She might

have pointed out to her that they were dating but something about hearing Selena call her "girlfriend" flipped the heck out of her stomach. In the best way ever.

Selena's grin got bigger until she buried her face in her arm and groaned. "I miss you and your hugs so much!" Her voice was almost a whine. Selena never whined. She was diligent and resilient. But knowing she felt the same kind of yearning June felt for her was so good to know.

"I'm rooting for you, Selena Clarke. You kick those demon asses." She raised her fist in a cheer.

"Yes, babe!" Selena proclaimed with a mirrored cheer. June beamed until a yawn nearly broke her face. "Aw, you're tired," Selena observed.

"It's mostly my body needing to crash. I had a long day at the salon."

"Stretch well, babe, and get a lot of rest. I'll see you Thursday. I've got the night off. If someone breaks into your place at around seven PM, know that it's me."

June smiled. "I love one burglar." She made a one with her free hand then let it fall onto Lemon who had basically began snoozing right on top of her stomach.

"Goodnight, darlin', dream of me!" Selena purred.

COME THURSDAY, JUNE HAD A BUSY ENOUGH DAY THAT she wasn't spending her entire day off staring at her phone and flipping through the spotlight story Selena used to post updates of her rehearsals.

She was practically swamped with books. Mid-April clean up got Bastoog and its employees bustling around. They'd spent the last two hours hauling new books and redesigning the face of the shop.

June was designated to the used books area. Due to their Spring deals, the place was kind of a mess. June didn't mind the work. She popped headphones in and got to work with the croon of one Marina. Her phone buzzed her out of arranging the Ps. She pulled her earbuds out and was transported back somewhere uncomfortable.

"Auntie, where are these supposed to go?" Shelby asked behind the pile of books in their arms. They were stacked so high; they couldn't possibly see much.

"Hey, let me help you with those."

"There's no need, I'm strong, Steven," Shelby dismissed him.

June heard her best friend's voice and looked up. Steve was the dude working for her mom for close to seven years now and he kind of was impossible to ignore. He had that deep voice people always assumed came with a lot of attitude and racism. But for a white guy, he was alright. Except for his incessant need to wear really hideous graphic t-shirts and cargo pants.

"Junie!" Shelby realized June's stare.

"Hey, you're going to hurt yourself," June murmured, and automatically grabbed some of the hardcovers Shelby had stacked until they didn't need to poke their head to the side to talk.

"How come you let her help and not me?"

"Because you're my rival and I won't lose in a game of strength."

Had June not known Shelby for a long time, she'd have thought they were serious, but despite the deadpan face and the no-nonsense look in their hazel eyes, they were mostly kidding.

Steve seemed to know that too. He chuckled. Which was a spectacle that included him throwing his head back.

Wow. Steve walked away, the pile in his arms kind of looking intimidating as heck. He headed towards the YA section.

The two took themselves to another section, which was the romance genre. June shelved one bare-chested cover after the other almost methodologically. She couldn't stop thinking of the text she got and the immediate drop of spirits she had. She'd always known her moods were dangerously susceptible to outside factors but feeling them change so quickly drained her. A tiny headache started pulsating behind one of her eyes and she suddenly wanted to be back on her couch watching something mindless.

"What's wrong?" Shelby asked quietly.

June shrugged.

"Come on, I can see it all over your face." They poked June's side with a paperback.

June heaved a big sigh which automatically made her feel melodramatic and even sadder. "Selena won't be able to pop in tonight. I... uh... haven't seen her in too long and I miss her."

Shelby dropped their eyebrows and frowned. "Is everything okay?"

"Yeah, yeah, she just needs to stay longer and kind of sacrifice her break to get this complicated action shot done. Her castmate is being exceptionally daft today." June itched to take out her phone again and send something else besides the "I UNDERSTAND<3!!" text.

Shelby still pursed their lip and looked at June.

"What?" June stopped shelving and looked at Shelby.

"What about you? Are you okay?"

"What do you mean? I'm fine," June dismissed.

"June. You and I both know you're... kind of..." they trailed off.

"Oh, come out with it, already, Shelbz," June said. There wasn't much Shelby could say about her that'd shock June but hearing the hesitance in their voice? Kind of freaky.

"You're attached," they said as they evaded June's eye contact.

"To Selena? I sure hope I am. I'm her girlfriend." She was close to rolling her eyes.

"Not that way. That's fine. I mean attached to your comforts. Why don't you drop by and surprise her? She probably wanted to see you as much as you wanted to see her," they reasoned.

"She'll probably be busy, though."

"So?"

"I don't wanna bug her, Shelbz."

Shelby rolled their eyes.

"You're letting anxiety talk, now. You know I hate that bitch."

"Oh, so now my anxiety is a bitch?"

"Sweetie, all anxieties are bitches. But we are anxiety's bitch so... we're not even the boss bitch," they explained with a wise look.

June's brain was gonna explode if she continued to listen to Shelby. But they were kind of... right.

The realization of Shelby's words and how reasonable they were being was kind of the opposite of June's expectation. She wasn't some egotistical person who thought she knew herself better than anyone else knew her. There was a shit ton in her brain she refused to face. She gave Shelby a look and continued to think.

They weren't wrong. Admitting that would give them some satisfaction though so June pettily kept it in her mind.

She should reciprocate and go see Selena. She'd missed

her the past week so much she'd began talking about her to anyone who'd listen. Her last appointment before she hurried to Bastoog had listened with a kind smile and patted her hand afterwards. Older ladies were so kind and didn't mind her nervous chatter.

June pleaded with her brain to stop overthinking and got her fingers working.

June: Is it okay if I stop by and see you?

She sent the text and put her phone back in her pocket. Shelby had a grin on their face when they saw her so June mimicked throwing a heavy paperback at them.

"You know I'm wise and all-knowing."

"Keep that ego from inflating, boo, this place isn't big enough," she retorted.

"Meh, I like it the size of the Empire State Building."

It was then that Steve had been walking by them and he took a sharp turn and gave Shelby a look. Shelby waved him off, but June saw the clear as day smile they hid. June wasn't one to look too much into things but—the buzz in her pocket startled her.

Selena: OMG RLY????

June: Yes! Send me your location!

Selena shared her location. Seeing how it'd take her at

least twenty minutes, June also saw how it approached six PM.

"Is that Selena? Am I right? Are you going to see her? Am I the genius who saved you from heartbreak?" they said in rapid-fire speech until June had to push them physically away as she laughed.

"Go away, Shelby, I have a girlfriend to woo!" she said a bit loudly that some patrons turned their heads to her. June fought the embarrassment and kept her head high.

Zahra was working the cashier then because even if she was retiring she just couldn't stop working. She saw June approach and raised an eyebrow. "Was that you I heard making a romantic gesture?"

"Yeah. Yes. It's me. I gotta go, Mama."

"Be safe," her mom murmured as she kissed June on the cheek.

It took June roughly an hour to get the things she had in mind together before she was stuck in semi-jammed traffic on her way to Selena's location. The sky was dark but when she got a special entrance tag, thank you Selena, and parked, it twinkled with some stars. June wasn't one for signs, but she'd take a couple of them over nothing in that moment. She hoisted the basket she put together closer to her chest and let her thighs take her there.

Selena didn't get a trailer, but she got a room to relax in. Thankfully, when June addressed the coordinator, the person seemed familiar with who June was.

"Hi, I'm Talia. Selena spoke to me about you showing up and I see you already got a guest badge!" Talia was perky and small. June couldn't help but smile at them. Her nerves kind of shut down her speech abilities.

She nodded in thanks as Talia led her to Selena's corner. The sounds of other people milling around, drinking coffee at nearly nine PM and shooting scenes were background noises. June applied her mom's advice of focusing on one thing when the world tried to overwhelm her.

The line of doors was easy to navigate. Selena's had Selena Clarke and her character's name "Ariel" in caps. June braced herself. For what? She had no clue. She knocked.

"Coming!" Selena's voice came a couple of seconds later.

The person answering the door to June's knock wasn't Selena really. What June could see from the blank tank-top, which didn't cover much of Selena's arms, was covered in black intertwining vines with flowers growing on the peak of Selena's shoulders and some leaves close to her neck. June knew they were done for the filming. Seeing Selena with her curls free and her makeup done minimally but still striking enough caused the butterflies in her stomach to go wild. And the contacts. She had hazel contacts on that made her eyes shine just enough.

"God," June whispered.

Selena's reaction was probably the cutest thing June had ever seen, though. She practically beamed so hard her dimples discovered new ways to blow the air out of June's lungs. If not for the basket so tightly held in June's arms, Selena might have crushed her in a hug. Stupid basket. June immediately put it down and wrapped her arms around Selena.

She was once again in the embrace of almonds and vanilla and if the tattoos, makeup, and wardrobe made her feel like she was looking at an ethereal stranger, the scent brought her back home.

"I knew you were coming but, gah, seeing you here is still so exciting," Selena gushed once she pulled June into her room. The place was small, with a fridge and a giant mirror and a rack of clothes. June assumed someone would be helping Selena change and stuff. She took a look at the place before Selena dragged her to the comfy couch with its side-table.

"Come here. I want some more hugs."

Selena's voice hitched a bit as if she'd felt as much yearning as June did. On second thought, she might have. June was more than happy to settle into the cushion and let Selena maneuver them around until June's thighs were bracketed by Selena's. She was a bit taller than her this way.

June looked up and again, the sight made the world quiet down.

"I've missed you," she murmured. Selena grinned at her and replied right into her lips. She kissed her with fervor. Anticipation be gone. Selena was all in. Lips moved so heatedly that June's very own fingertips went hot. She clutched onto Selena's tank top, pulled her into her chest and let their bellies, and their tits mash. She groaned when Selena bit into her lip and murmured something about her taste.

"Thanks, I had a muffin this morning."

"Wait? This morning? It's nine p.m., babe." Selena gave her a look, her hands clutching June's shoulders.

June looked away, kind of embarrassed but also so extremely pleased Selena worried over her. It was complicated.

"That's okay, I'll ask Talia to order us something. I'll call her now. What do you feel like eating? Pizza? Pasta? Sandwiches? Just fries?"

Selena talked so fast and was pushing herself off June's lap to get her phone. June automatically grabbed onto Selena's hips, by the belt loops. She worried for a nanosecond she was going to tear them off Selena's black skin-tight jeans but with Selena back in her lap, her mouth on hers, and nothing but the sound of their soft moans in her ears, June did not give one fuck.

June's hands found their way to Selena's thighs. The jeans were really excellent because with every caress from her, Selena squirmed and sighed into June's mouth. Selena's hands on the base of her neck might have tightened around some of her hair which made June's own stomach flare up with heat. She massaged the thick thighs, trailed her hands higher and higher until she grasped the hips she'd adored for so long in her palms. She tried her best not to tickle Selena, but the touch still made Selena chuckle. Selena wasn't too distracted to slip her tongue into June's mouth, though, which was great.

The taste of Selena on her tongue, the sweat gathering from how hotly their chests connected. The hand in her hair, gripping tight enough to make June crane her neck and pant directly into Selena's neck.

Selena pulled back, and with a grin, kind of dangerous and a hell lot of sexy, leaned in and nipped June's ear.

The electricity in June transferred to one spot under her stomach and it made her so tingly she just couldn't help slipping her hands under Selena's tank top. The cream of her back, the light dusting of hair that was barely visible, the arch of her back when Selena pulled away to groan. They made stars show up right there in June's eyes.

"You're so beautiful."

Selena's smile was so shy and sweet then that June wanted to eat her up.

"Is this okay?" June asked.

Selena tilted her head to the side. "Do you mean if I'm sexually attracted to you right now?"

There wasn't a hint of sarcasm on Selena's voice, which helped calm June's worry that she was being too direct. She nodded.

Selena smiled beautifully and nodded as well. "It feels good. But not like I'm in a hurry to like... come or anything. It's fun and hot."

June grinned. "Same."

Selena's eyes dropped to half-mast and she resumed her torturous kissing and nipping of June's ear. June also felt good and unhurried. The wave of heat took over her but not in an overwhelming way. She enjoyed it. When Selena pulled away, June's eyes fell to the rise of her chest. There was a lovely rose on her chest, and it gave June all kinds of ideas of bites.

"Can I bite you?" she murmured, and Selena's lashes fluttered.

"Depends?" She sounded so sweet, whispering close to June's ear.

"On?" June's fingers traced Selena's spine and it made the girl arch back.

"My girlfriend might mind?" Selena said with a laugh.

"Oh, yeah?" June nuzzled Selena's neck, bringing her close to her mouth.

"And my agent."

"Fuck that." Selena's curls blanketed them from the world, making the sparkle in Selena's eyes so much lovelier. June wanted to see nothing but Selena.

"Mmmm, yes, fuck my agent."

June laughed. "No, not like that."

Selena smiled dreamily and nipped June's mouth.

"I think your girlfriend would understand if I put my teeth on you." Selena's hips bucked against June's, making her wish she hadn't changed out of her sweatpants.

"I think so too. But again, where? Somewhere I'll need to cover up with makeup?"

"Not... exactly," June replied, and Selena's eyes widened. "Not anywhere under the belt," June clarified with a grin. Selena poked her tongue out playfully.

"Oh my god, June, are you saying you want to bite my tits?"

"I was gonna go for your belly— ouch," June laughed at the playful swat of Selena's hands.

"Tease." The pout on her full lips, well-kissed and shiny with spit, made June want to do it even more.

With a grin and a hiked-up eyebrow, her best impression of Flynn Rider, June whispered, "Can I bite your tits, babe?" June expected giggly Selena, but she didn't expect her to outright lean back and remove her tank-top in what was an incomparably the hottest move ever.

Under the tank-top was a gauzy contraption that framed Selena's tits so gorgeously, it would be a crime to remove it. June didn't have to.

With her eyes locked onto Selena's, watching the flare of her nostrils and the half-lidded look she gave her, June wrapped her teeth lightly somewhere above the seam of the bra and bit. Selena's moan was so lovely, but she covered it up by biting into her lower lip. June soothed the spot with her tongue and when Selena's hands came to her jaw and pulled her for a kiss, she leaned into her mouth.

She loved Selena's reactions. The hitched breaths. The heaving chest. The little sounds that June wasn't sure Selena knew she let out. She loved them so much she wanted to see more. But, June knew, in the deep pit of her mind, she wasn't ready. And that was okay.

When their mouths got a bit worn out from kissing and June's stomach growled with hunger, Selena pulled away and pecked June's cheek.

"I'm glad you got to feast on me, but you need to eat real food."

"You can be real food," June mumbled.

"Are you saying you'd give up pizza for me? You'd give up pickles?" Selena asked with a skeptical look. June thought about it.

"Yep."

"Babe, I love you but don't ever do that for me."

June's breath practically exited the building and she sat there, with Selena in her lap, in her hands, smiling down at her like an angel.

"Wait, did you just say what I think I heard you say?"

Selena's mouth pursed but then, as if she couldn't help it, she smiled wide and bright.

"Yep. I love you."

June's eyes betrayed her then by watering. She swallowed the chunk of emotion in her throat and croaked, "I love you too."

There weren't fireworks. There wasn't an audience applauding. There was just June and Selena, holding one another, breathing in tandem, and there were their hearts, plain and in sight. And in love.

"I love you so much I'm going to call your mom on you if you don't eat," Selena murmured. She kissed June.

"I love you so much that's why I packed us some of your favorit—"

"Shawarma?" Selena practically squealed.

"With extra taheena and pickles."

"Oh my god, I think I love you... ten percent more."

June laughed and hugged her close. She didn't want to let go of anything in that moment. Not the quiet certainty, not the warmth against her cheek, not the living evidence that June's found something so irreplaceable.

The abandoned basket finally got some attention. Selena got the food out with the carefully placed cans of peach iced tea, which was Selena's favorite flavor, and the extra tissues as well as a small bag filled with other stuff.

"Junie, you got me face masks?" Selena sounded amazed as if she didn't probably own and get hundred dollars' worth of skin care and makeup in endorsements.

"I just remembered you liked this brand when you tried it at my place, so," June trailed off.

Selena gathered her palms to her chest and gave June a dreamy happy smile that made June want to kiss it on Selena's face. Selena also found a whole jar of pickles that June had to insist she take and munch on whenever she needed the salty treat.

"This is quite the care package."

June shrugged and stuffed her face with Shawarma. She really wasn't the best at taking compliments, but she let the sunshine radiating off Selena's joy and love wash over her. (Her heart still rejoiced at the fact she was loved).

There was still the topic of how June got the courage to make her move. To finally try and step out for Selena. She cleared her throat to get Selena's attention since she'd been trying to open the jar of pickles.

Selena looked up with a quirked eyebrow. She was quite focused.

"Well, someone wise, I won't mention who—"

"Is it Shelby?" Selena grinned.

"Gah, did they get you to say this?" June huffed but she wasn't actually bothered.

Selena chuckled. "Nah, but I have a feeling they act as your conscience sometimes."

"Anyway, so Shelby kind of brought up a really good point today as I stared at our texts. I'm kind of insulted they did it so succinctly, by the way, but yeah, they think I've been kind of getting too comfortable in how I expect you to be the one to initiate. And I—" she held a hand up when she saw Selena open her mouth. "I just want to get this out, please." Selena nodded and closed her mouth.

"I agree with Shelby. It's not bad that I feel comfortable with you. It's one of the things I adore about us. One of the things I love about *you*. You make me feel good being myself. I am never trying to be someone funnier or more interesting.

"However, I want to put more effort to get out of my comfort zone. I want to be there for you when you're so busy. I want you to be able to tell me to come to you. I want to be your comfort as much as you are mine. And I want to try being your girlfriend offline and online."

Selena's eyes had widened but then softened. She put her food down and motioned for June to do the same. She took her hands and rubbed her thumbs across June's knuckles.

When she began to talk, her voice was soft, but it got confident as she went on. Not once did she take her hands out from June's grip.

"I knew I felt something for you the minute I shook your hand. I felt companionship and I felt care. You make me feel so much and so evidently. I am never worried around you.

"In a way, June, you have become a comfort for me.

Exciting. Full of feel-good fluffy moments. I don't mind that I come to you. But you coming to me... like today? I wouldn't say no to that at all. And to try out being public? It means so much. Thank you. For trusting me to be there for you and for allowing me to be myself too."

Her words got a bit choked up right there at the end. June's own eyes might have gotten a bit blurry to match. They were a bunch of sap gals and it was honestly great. June leaned to give Selena a quick kiss.

"Yum, pickles," she hummed. Selena giggled and stole another kiss.

"Gah, I can't believe Shelby is going to lord this over me forever. They're gonna be insufferable." June rolled her eyes exaggeratedly.

"Good. I'm so glad we got someone like them in our corner, cheering us on," Selena replied.

Speaking of Shelby, June's phone buzzed, a familiar all caps question of: "DID Y'ALL HAVE A HUGE ROMANTIC MOMENT???"

June groaned, but Selena laughed herself until tears showed up at the corner of her eyes.

"We're so smitten. Couldn't even last a week without you," Selena murmured.

"Is it me or my cats?"

"*You* always but please don't tell Lemint I said that," Selena whispered, as if the cats would show up.

"Ah! Lemint, I love that! It'll be their ship title!"

"Just like how ours will be... Jelena?" Selena suggested.

"Babe that's just a J instead of an S in your whole name," June deadpanned.

Selena opened her mouth but got interrupted by a knock. It was Talia telling her she had a line rehearsal. It must have been glaringly obvious that the two had been through *something* and the grin on Talia's face made June's blush flare up.

"Thanks so much, T, I'll make sure I'm there in five minutes."

"Excellent! Pleased to meet you again, June!" She waved and ran off. June had her hand up in a half-wave as Selena gave her a quirked smiled.

"Do you think everyone knows about us being sappy as heck in here?"

"Not yet." June didn't even want to hide the blush. It was a sign of her body loving Selena. She'd wear it with honor.

EPILOGUE

Selena checked herself in the front facing camera. Lipstick as red as possible? Check. Her hair bouncy and fluffy? Check. Her dress floral and off-shoulder? Check.

She was armed to the teeth with all things that made her feel good and beautiful. She changed apps to Instagram and started the live stream she promised her followers. In a couple of minutes people started to pour into the live, sending her hearts, questions about what she was up to, and what was the cute thing happening.

It had been Selena's own words that hyped her followers so much. She'd posted a picture on her feed with a secret message that she and June had worked on for a very long time. June even talked to her therapist about the whole being public thing. And after a good couple of months of procrastinating the news, they decided that they'd reveal their relationship to Selena's followers in the most casual of ways: with deflection.

She'd been sitting in June's tiny couch, with Lemon purring in her lap and the sun shining through the window. The mid-august sun was so refreshing on her skin.

"Hey everyone. I'm so glad so many of y'all could catch this live!" She made sure to keep her voice steady enough so that her nerves wouldn't show. June promised her she'd be cool about it, but Selena still wanted to be the rock that June could rely on.

"What I'm about to do is reveal the date of when The Huntress is going to premier! But before that, I am going to need my girlfriend to bring me my sandwich!" she gave the camera a wink just as June came back to the couch with said sandwiches. The very mention of the word *girlfriend* got her followers buzzing.

Girlfriend????
Holy shit Selena is seeing someone???
Sapphic queen!!!!
Reveal to us ur wife

The comments were amusing enough and came so quickly that even when she turned the screen to June, they couldn't read them fast enough.

It didn't help that the second June showed in the frame, they got wilder. June smiled her half-smirk half-smile and gave the camera a salute. She full on grinned when Selena groaned.

"See the level of cool I have to handle every day?" Selena told her fans.

June shrugged and said nothing. Since June already warned her that anxiety made her clamp up, Selena didn't worry too much. She just grinned at her blushing girlfriend and gave her a wink when she landed a kiss to her shoulder.

Which, she probably shouldn't have done. The chaos that erupt in the chat was dizzying. But Selena couldn't care too much.

She saw the easy grin on June's face and remembered the strength her girl had shown every step of their relationship. Being in the face of the public with Selena right now must not be a big deal to others but to June, it was a big deal. But she believed that June would excel at everything she put her mind to.

"Junie, wanna help me reveal the Huntress' date?" Selena kept her eyes on June. June quirked a lip and leaned back, taking a bite of her sandwich. She shrugged.

Selena turned to the camera. And for a minute, marveled over their reflection. Two soft round-faced gals, grinning from ear to ear. "Junie gets nervous. Anyway, Junie had the opportunity to work personally on one of my all-time best looks on the show which you'll see so soon!"

June put down her sandwich and after wiping her mouth from crumbs, gave Selena a look.

"Babe, you make my job so easy with you being gorgeous," June murmured. It was low, but it made the blood in Selena's veins heat and the comments to go wild. Go figure that they loved June.

"Alright, sweeties, the date for The Huntress' first episode which will air online and have its first premier is... drum roll, please," she directed that at June. June grinned and drummed her thighs. "September 10th!"

"You heard it, sweets. September 10 is the date where y'all will get to see me--"

"Kick ass!" June exclaimed. Selena laughed.

"Kick ass and more! I'm just so excited for everyone to see this. It's my first project in which a girl like me: black, queer, and fat is going to be the lead. I had so much fun and many grueling months working on perfecting this role to be something everyone would be proud of. I would like to thank everyone for being so supportive. And my own family who had to handle my whiny ass whenever I got a sore back."

June laughed at that and Selena wiggled her brows. She hoped that wasn't too suggestive. It reminded her of two weeks ago when they wrapped up the filming and Selena took June to meet her family.

Selena knew it'd be chaotic. She practically counted on her sisters to ask June about everything and for her mother to stuff mashed potatoes thick with sauce, veggies and meat into her mouth. June somehow had managed it. She was graceful, and she was great with the little gremlins who called Selena auntie.

By ten p.m. that night, when June sank into the seat of Selena's car, a tired smile on her face and a gleam in her eyes, Selena had felt assured. She remembered her mom's words. "She's a keeper," she said as she looked out the kitchen window where June had three of Selena's nieces in her arms and was twirling them around until they screamed with mirth.

Selena had leant over and pecked June's mouth right there in the car because fuck driving to the airport. June had hummed and pulled her for a longer kiss.

Selena got pulled back to the present, which made her wonder even more how many surprises await her with this girl by her side. A girl who saw her soul, and got her breath quickening in all the good ways she'd thought weren't for her.

"Anyway, more news will come out and I'll make sure y'all are up to date! Don't forget to give my co-stars a lot of support, love, and comments! This show has so much diversity, heart, familial love, and monsters!"

"And the badasses who fight them," June added.

Selena grinned at her.

Seeing the freckles, darker than they'd been in February, due to the tan June got from the summer's sun, the pink in her round cheeks, and her no-makeup glory, made Selena lean in for a kiss. She was so weak to those lips.

June closed her eyes and brought her hand up to Selena's jaw, tilting her head to get more of her taste.

Without looking, Selena ended the Live and let her mind get fuzzy with all the good feelings and the taste of her beloved.

The End

A GIFT FROM MINA

Turn the page for an Extra Soft scene.

Rated E for explicit portrayal of sex between two consenting women.

EXTRA SOFT

Light particles shined through the little spaces in the curtains. They were creamy and had pink lace at the bottom, which didn't touch the floor. If June knew one thing it was to buy accurately sized curtains. First, she had two cats whose hair got...everywhere, which led to second, she hated the sight of dirty curtains.

She stepped back after setting the last paperback onto the white bookshelf. The room was spacious and had little corners where June personalized her bookshelf and Selena had picture frames on the wall.

June could not believe she now lived with her girlfriend.

They'd taken on different rooms of the apartment they now leased together. It was closer to June's mom's apartment above the bookstore and the salon where she part-timed. It also meant June no longer needed to use a car. The car sale went toward starting up a new project at Bastoog, which June knew Shelby had been excited about.

A creak in the floorboards told June that Selena was still in the kitchen. The place wasn't extravagant, but Selena and June's paychecks allowed them comfort. It was a two-bedroom place. They set up very humble guest room which also doubled as June's makeup room. It was where her freelancing happened outside the salon.

Lemon and Mint had tried their best to take over it. Selena was the weak one when it came to denying the cats. She'd take one look at Mint's eyes and just let him in. Not that June was any better at turning them down. That meant Selena and June had to schedule weekly grooming sessions for Lemon to keep his hair from coating everything in the apartment.

It was what Shelby named a fun family activity. Last time they showed up, Selena had been cooing Lemon as June took on the mission of untangling his hair and using the fancy coat spray to make his hair shine. In the end, he cuddled Selena and gave June the silent treatment. Shelby watched from the couch with Mint in their lap, accepting lots and lots of ear scratches.

That was their life for now.

A bubble of literal joy manifested in June's chest whenever she'd think of their little set up.

It was unlike everything she'd ever imagined for herself.

It was better.

Unpacking, though, was exhausting. Between the two of them, it took close to three weeks thanks to Selena's busy schedule promoting her show and June's work schedule. They would do a minimum of unpacking one day at a time and collapse into soft cuddles, kisses and snoozes swiftly every night.

June was for once free for the day and devoted her morning to setting up the bedroom. She'd been staring at the empty walls and decided: nope. No can do. Selena's previous apartment had been chic but unlived in. So, June wanted Selena to feel entirely at home with June. Thanks to working on the bookstore with her mama, June knew her way around tools.

It hadn't taken her long to hang up the frames then slip in the pictures that Selena had meticulously chosen. By the bed was a framed photo of them on that trip to Mrs. Clarke's place. Selena's sister Amy had taken it.

It was of the two of them at dinner. They'd been occupied with gazing into one another's eyes and holding hands rather than eating. The porch had been backlit with fairy light—which clued June in on where exactly Selena's love for fairy lights—and the candles on the table helped illuminate their faces. Mrs. Clarke's food was homey and delicious in every bite. June remembered the ease with which she navigated the trip. She remembered looking at Selena's clear dark eyes, lashed and glimmering in the low light and thinking, "I want to spend my life loving you."

It didn't hurt to have a photo of the exact moment June Bana knew she wanted to marry Selena one day.

June had turned to her boxes of books and began hauling them to the shelves. That took approximately three hours because she got distracted with her favorite romance paperbacks, which were deeply loved and reread until they showed it.

She even began rereading a specific book concerning a lost modern-day black princess. With one last chapter about the dreamy confused princess, June put it on the shelf and continued her work.

When she finally was satisfied with the bedroom, June could feel the sweat gathered under her boobs. She definitely deserved a long shower.

June headed to the en suite bathroom. It was perfectly sized. With a tub that comfortably contained Selena for her weekly pampering sessions. It made for a spacious shower for June to feel refreshed in.

When she left the bathroom a bit steamer than it was, June found Selena perched on the bed. With the framed photo of them in her hands. Her hair was in its braids for maximum efficiency and had a crop top on with a pair of leggings.

"Hey, babe," June murmured as she adjusted the wrapped towel on her head.

Selena looked up, her forehead shone with sweat. She must have been working very hard on getting the kitchen all tidied up. A surge of love washed over June and she hurried to sit next to Selena.

The bed gave under her weight, bringing her closer into Selena's warmth. June could feel the water from her hair drip down the side of her face and while usually she'd do a better job drying her hair, she couldn't care less. She wanted to bask in the glory of Selena looking all soft.

"Hey," she replied. Selena had a dazed kind of look. And it was directed to June's collar. June's bathrobe must have gotten loose on her. June knew the blush was spreading up from her chest, to her neck and further to her cheeks.

"Like what you're seeing?" June teased. Selena's eyes fluttered up to look at June's and she licked her lower lip.

"If I say yes, would you be cool with that?" Selena's voice sounded so hesitant June's heart took a leap.

"I'd be absolutely cool with that." June leaned in. She kissed Selena's neck. It made Selena shudder and reach out to hold June's hands. They'd been on June's thighs.

The thought of Selena's hands so close to her inner thighs made June sigh at the contact. She kissed and nipped Selena's jaw which made Selena groan lightly. It was softly rounded, and June absolutely adored it. But she also wanted to get to that mouth. The mouth that made June think of sweetness mingled with Selena's happy sighs.

When June pulled away, she saw Selena's eyes screwed up and her breaths coming in fast inhalations. They made Selena's chest move up and down. June wanted to bottle up every movement in her mind.

Selena opened her eyes and what she found in June's eyes loosened Selena's grip on June's hands.

"I—I think I better get back to the kitchen." Selena made to get up and disappointment felt like a boulder in June's stomach. Thoughts of them naked, sweaty, and satisfied were deflating.

Unless.

"Ughhhh," June groaned as she threw herself back at the queen-sized bed. The bed June knew Selena had spent a meticulous time making that morning. Selena turned from the door to give June an excitingly tentative look over her shoulder. Until Selena saw what June was planning to do to the bed.

"Hey! Don't mess that up, it looks too good to even sleep in," Selena said with very little heat about the actual bed. June saw how Selena eyed the bathrobe, which opened a little to reveal a long stretch of June's thigh.

"I bet we can do more than just sleep in it." June wiggled her brows. She slipped a hand to said exposed thigh and fingered the fringe of the robe. Selena's throat moved as she swallowed. Then she looked at June in the eyes and smirked.

"Oh yeah? Like what?" Selena put both hands on her hips and watched June fumble. June suddenly felt like a novice at this seduction thing.

"I dunno. Like... eat nachos and get sauce on these pretty covers?" June shrugged.

Selena gasped in shock. "Fuck no! These are like super special bed covers."

"They're just floral, babe. You got like twelve floral sets," June argued. She felt a laugh bubbling inside her. It helped her nerves that they both were extremely aware of how June trailed her fingertips up and down her thigh, exposing more of it as she went. She saw Selena's fingers twitch. *Good, I want your hands on me. Hungry and demanding.*

"I can't believe you said *just floral*! It's like I don't know who you are anymore." Selena tried so hard to look hurt but while she was suppressing her urge to smile her body betrayed her. Her mouth curled naturally, and her eyes twinkled like two suns.

Selena tried at stern again, "These are lavender. You know how I feel about lavender."

"I'm starting to get very very jealous of the color and that might be the most ridiculous I've felt my whole life."

June accompanied her words with untying her bathrobe. The ache between her thighs felt nearly impossible to ignore. There were clear signs of arousal on her; her breath quickening and her pupils dilating, which were obvious even at the little distance they had between them.

But, Selena didn't move closer, even when June's robe revealed a long stripe of her hip. June made sure she left some of the robe to cover her pussy. June didn't want Selena to feel pressured to act on her desires.

The sight moved Selena. She took one step, and at that second, Selena's frown gave away to amusement in every inch of her wide smile. She didn't say a word, just merely devoured the sight of June leaning back on her elbows, offering her freshly bathed body to any sampling Selena wished to partake in.

June felt impatience climb her skin, goose bumps rose, and she shivered a little. She nodded at Selena and said, "Come here. Lemme prove that I'm better than lavender."

Selena raised a hand to the edge of her crop top. It was floral, and bright yellow. It made her brown skin glow so nicely June wondered if her tongue would burn if she licked Selena's tummy. Her beautiful soft stomach which was currently very bare and tempting.

"Are you trying to seduce me?" Selena's voice was all messed up and airy.

"Is it working?" June tilted her head to the side, let a drop of water drip down her neck and chest. It was awkward, but she owned her sexuality, and was thoroughly invested in Selena seeing her enthusiasm.

Selena's eyes followed every movement, including the way June opened her legs, as if to welcome her between them.

She breathed heavily and said, "Absolutely."

She finally moved to place a knee on the bed, which was high enough to accommodate her. It put Selena much closer to June than before, which was a relief and a curse. June felt the heat radiating off her girlfriend and wished for nothing more than to be engulfed and eaten up entirely.

When Selena began to crawl on all fours over the soft floral covers she loved so much and painstakingly chose for their bed, June's chest felt like it was about to explode with love. Selena stopped with her knees on the side of June's hips, her ass brushed June's nearly exposed crotch and it made June want to buck and bring their bodies together, but she held back.

She made her move, it was Selena's turn.

But it didn't help that the move put her girlfriend's gorgeous tits right there for June to ogle and she just loved them. It was such a *power* move. With a sigh, June fisted the covers under her and looked into Selena's eyes.

The model knew her effect. She probably saw it in the helpless sighs June let out at every brush of their chests. Her thighs were so close and so lovely, and June couldn't touch. Not yet.

In that position, when Selena looked down, June might have had a tiny heart attack at how befitting the situation was to some of her fantasies.

She also, very clearly, was giving June a look that very obviously said, *how's this for seduction?* And June's mouth quirked in a grin.

"Okay, so now it is *you* who is seducing *me?*" she wondered aloud, and Selena grinned.

"What do you think, Junie? Is me crawling on top of you hot enough?" She brought her hand to her own stomach, making June's breath come so fast she worried she might panic. Like in many situations where June nearly panicked, she looked at Selena's eyes and timed her breaths with her.

"Fuck. Yeah. Absolutely." She reached up to hold onto Selena's hips, her favorite handles, but Selena swatted her hands away.

"Hands by your sides, please," she said beautifully with a kind smile.

June's eyes widened, and she put her hands back next to her hips. "Can I ask why?"

"Yeah. I want to..." Selena leaned down. The next words fanned over June's mouth, "finger myself right in front of you until you beg to suck my come soaked fingers into your mouth."

June's thighs quivered at the heat that shot through her lower half. *Holy shit.* Her hands went back to fisting the covers. She was *so* going to piss Selena off by ripping them off.

"Would that be something you'd like?" Selena asked. Her face betrayed caution and June found solace in knowing that her girlfriend was enthusiastic and hot for her.

"Yeah, babe, knock yourself out. Anything that makes you flush hot is good by me." June replied breathily. Her mouth was dry, and she knew licking her lips wouldn't help but it was nice to see Selena's eyes flash when she did.

As if in retaliation for being sexy, Selena placed her index finger, slowly, from blunt fingertip to the root, in her mouth. June saw her tongue twirl around the finger and imagine it on her skin, on her pussy and moaned.

"Two of us can be teases, you know," Selena said around her finger. She placed a second finger in her mouth, this time her middle finger, which was chubbier, and June's mind wanted to blank at the thought of it inside her. She whimpered.

"Selena," she repeated her name until Selena took mercy on her and placed the fingers on June's half-parted mouth. Gladly, June sucked them in and let the heat in her eyes eat up Selena. She was so lovely and decadent, and June wanted her taste saved in her mouth.

Her fingers tasted like skin, slightly salty and every suck of June's mouth made Selena's mouth let out a soft moan. She placed her free hand on her hips and without dislodging her fingers from June's slobbery sucking mouth, she pushed her leggings lower until the stretchy material unveiled the sight of cotton blue panties that looked so soft against Selena's brown skin. June's mouth opened, slack, and Selena's fingers slipped out, tracing wetness across

June's lip before the hand went to the edge of Selena's panties and slipped in.

With a groan, June realized she was going to come just from wanting her girlfriend to slip the very fingers that were in her mouth into her cunt. Selena's body rippled in a shudder as her hand slipped under the cotton. June's mouth watered even more at the sight of her fingers pushing against the material. It was such a scene that she could feel wetness between her thighs. She wanted more than nothing to be the one with her hands in Selena's panties. But she enjoyed the show.

Especially as it had Selena fluttering her lashes, her hand working so slowly that June admired her tenacity. With every rub of her fingers against, what June presumed was her clit, Selena's chest huffed, her tits shook, and June went back to daydreaming of the taste of Selena's skin on her tongue.

"Fuck, babe," June murmured as the hands she kept obediently next to her side went back to ferociously gripping the covers.

It didn't help that Selena opened her eyes and looked June straight on as she pushed her hands deeper into her panties. She let out a long whimper which might have had June's name in there. It made June's body flush from head to toe.

"Please, Selena, please," she mumbled as she threw her head back and groaned. She didn't know what she wanted. Selena's cunt against her mouth, her fingers curling inside her girlfriend, and making her shut her legs against her head, or did she want to suck a hickey into Selena's sternum as she milked her orgasms.

With one final hump in the air, Selena pulled out her

fingers. They looked even wetter than before and she trailed them against her belly, leaving a gloss on her skin.

June whimpered and leaned closer tentatively and when Selena nodded, she kissed the trail of wet from Selena's lower belly to her belly button. She stopped her tongue right where the crop top ended, and Selena's skin started. She was indeed very hot and flushed. It made sweat break out on June's body in a fresh coat.

This was a thing from her fantasies. When June would lie back in her bed and listen to Selena guide her into an orgasm until the two were huffing and chuckling at how much fun it was to come together.

But this didn't even compare.

This was heaven and sin all together. The taste of Selena mixing with her almond and vanilla body wash made June's mind fizz. Did June sneak a hand into her panties and rub herself silly just to the thought of Selena's taste on her tongue? Absolutely. Did she feel as if she'd die if she didn't have it right then? Absolutely.

Selena watched her suck her way back down until her back ached from the strain. She huffed, and Selena helpfully stretched out before her, offering herself with her half-lidded look and licking her bottom lip as if she were imagining June's tongue exactly where her fingers were.

June was losing patience.

"Babe, can I top you now?"

Selena's eyes fluttered open. She'd been humming as June's tongue slipped against the very bottom of her tits.

"Yeah, please."

June was good at taking commands and was even better at fulfilling whispered pleas.

The flip was surprisingly easy to do, and it left them

both grinning and chuckling breathlessly until June's bathrobe was shrugged off.

They'd never been entirely naked around one another. It just never was a thing and so June felt all kinds of insecure before Selena's hand went to her chin and brought her face closer.

They kissed chastely as if they weren't both on the verge of humping half naked (and fully naked in June's case). Selena's mouth curled in a smile and June leaned back to kiss her cheek, her jaw, and down her neck. Her top was still on, which was a no-no.

Instead of simply taking it off, June had an idea. A payback of some sort.

She traced the very edge of the top and got a finger-tip to graze Selena's nipple. She knew that she wasn't wearing a bra.

June's touch was light against the skin there and kept her eyes on Selena's face. The barely-there touch made her girl roll her lips into her mouth and groan.

"Tease. June Bana, you're a huge tease." She was breathless.

"I know," she mumbled, then realized, teasing was fun, but she also wanted to make Selena come. So, she stripped her from the top and watched Selena's tits shake with the sudden movement. She also might have tweaked her nips a little. Just to watch Selena's head get thrown back and her breath hitch.

"Fuck," she whispered.

When Selena looked back at her, her eyes smoldered. She was hungry for June.

With her tits now just begging for June's mouth, June didn't want to keep her lover waiting. She leaned forward and closed her mouth against the skin just close to Selena's nipple. But not quite. Selena's groan was so worth it.

She moved down her body, giving her belly light kisses that made Selena look at her with heart-eyes. It was very lovely until June got to Selena's panties.

"These gotta go," she murmured, and Selena nodded. She helped her take them off with the leggings in one go by lifting her hips.

June didn't want to make this any more nerve-racking for Selena as it might be in her head. A first time could be intense and good. She placed her hands around Selena's hips and kissed her mound. It had a nice trimmed bush, and she didn't really care. It was her first time between anyone's legs besides her own. She wasn't choosy. She just wanted to please her girl.

Selena's thighs pushed to close a bit when June kissed down her folds. She shuddered but was held back from shying away. June placed her arms against Selena's thighs to keep them open for her. The sight was so beautiful her mouth watered.

Directly onto Selena's cunt. The cool spit made Selena hiss and buck. Which brought her to June. It was a feast. June dug in.

She'd read a lot about this, but she knew actually eating Selena out would be different, and from the heavy thump of her heart, like fucking drums in her chest, she knew this already was.

June tried her best to take her time, to lick and suck lightly, to tease out all the lovely huffs and puffs from Selena's mouth but she herself got impatient. She wanted to have her grind down in helplessness.

She wanted Selena to lose some of her famous control.

June might be a virgin, but she was an expert on masturbation and it worked just perfectly that her girlfriend was vocal and expressive.

There was one way to do that. June raised herself and with it, Selena's pelvis. This gave her advantage to just close her mouth against Selena's clit and lick. She moved her tongue in accordance to what made Selena's juices flow faster, what made her fingers on her own thighs tighten.

When she felt Selena's whole body clench up, June pulled back.

The sob of frustration that came from Selena was gorgeous.

"Not yet," June murmured, and Selena huffed.

"Of course, you'd try and edge me. You're terrible," she murmured lovingly.

June grinned and when Selena's body began to relax, she went back to work.

"Yeah, yeah, lick me harder," Selena instructed. June looked up and as she pressed the flat of her tongue against Selena's clit, she gave her girl what she wanted.

Selena's groan was ninety percent her name and ten perfect a shout. June felt her own cunt throb with the need to be touched. But first, Selena had to be wrecked.

As if reading June's agenda, Selena pressed her hands in her hair and pushed her face against her. The stroke of her tongue, her lips teasing Selena's lips apart, licking her until the pearly come was all she could taste and smell, it was a blessed union, really.

Then she did it again. She stopped just as Selena was about to come. She felt the tightening around her tongue, which made Selena curse her out.

"Come on, babe, I need you."

The words were so lovely but June merely grinned and kissed Selena's lower lips.

"I'm just giving you a good time, babe."

"Please," Selena whispered and June's resolve to tease her broke a little. She nodded and licked a long stripe from Selena's vagina to her clit.

She had Selena's nipple in her fingers as her tongue twirled and licked until she quite heard Selena's whine. "I need more," she told June.

"What do you need, baby? Tell me,"

Selena's eyes opened a bit wider at how low and deep June's voice had gone. She smirked, and she swore that Selena bucked harder against her.

"Please. Please."

"Use your words, baby."

"Fuck, June, please."

"I won't know what to do if you don't boss me around."

Selena's eyes narrowed but she had a soft smile on her mouth. June turned her head to nip at Selena's inner thigh. It made the girl whine and shudder. Her cunt also looked so ripe June just went back to it. She was falling in love with the taste of Selena's pussy.

"Fuck me, fuck me," she repeated with a moan and her hands were demanding and scratching June's shoulders. It was genius of her.

June quickly put her middle finger in her mouth, lubricating it like she did Selena's and eased it into her cunt.

It was so warm and wet that June felt no obstruction. She slipped as far as it'd go and watched Selena squirm for more. She pushed on June's hand and June eased another finger in. This time, Selena groaned and huffed.

"Better?" she asked.

Selena's eyes were like embers, dark and on fire, when she opened her eyes. "You're not fucking me yet," she whined.

"As you wish," June replied with a grin and she curled her fingers. She had a specific technique and wanted to learn every tick and give of Selena's hips. She wanted to know all there was to know about how to make Selena come. She rocked her fingers inside, curling them as they teased Selena's g-spot. June's mouth went back to its favorite snack and made Selena thrash in the bed she was protecting from getting messy. June closed her eyes and lost herself in her senses. She felt so loved between Selena's thighs. With every moan and whispered, "God, Junie, baby," June's mind ate it up.

Apparently, Selena liked to cry when she orgasmed. Tears overflowed as Selena's body heaved and twitched. It was an experience and made June crawl up Selena's body after giving her cunt a tiny lick that made Selena's sob come out more choked out than before.

"Come here," Selena whispered, and June found herself hugged to ample bosoms.

"I love you," she murmured.

Selena pulled her back, hands gentle against her cheeks.

She kissed June deeply, tasting herself probably on June's tongue.

June heard Selena's whispered, "I love you" and smiled.

"But I'm going to make you cry too," she added with a mouth full of sin. June couldn't wait.

ACKNOWLEDGMENTS

To my amazing cats Latte and Blue who have been there for me since day one by stepping on my keyboard and freaking the heck out of me. You're my true troopers.

To everyone on Twitter who liked, retweeted, and made me believe that this story could be told. Thank you.

To Shelby Eileen for listening to my rambling one day about two fat girls who are soft and deserving of happiness. Us fatty virgos must stick together.

To Shafiq Shaar, who I've annoyed tremendously and who drew the perfect soft cover. You've nagged me even when I wanted to block your texts. Thanks for the push, I needed it.

To my beta readers.

To my editor Mel who was great help.

To romance writers of color who inspire me. And especially Talia Hibbert. Every fat heroine of yours played a role in me gaining some semblance of confidence.

Thank you.

ABOUT MINA WAHEED

Mina grew up on TV and K-pop like many in their generation. At thirteen, they picked up their first book with the blessing of an older sister and has been in love with prose ever since.

They learned a lot about how to be a hermit and not interact with people, but love hearing from readers! Reach Mina through social media or email if you're shy like them.

 twitter.com/minawaheedrom

instagram.com/minawaheedrom

Made in the USA
Monee, IL
02 December 2022

19385906R00104